SPACER

SPACER, SMUGGLER, PIRATE, SPY — BOOK I

J A SUTHERLAND

DARKSPACE PRESS

SPACER
Spacer, Smuggler, Pirate, Spy — Book I

by J.A. Sutherland

Part I was originally published as the short story

WRONGED
A Story of the Dark

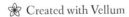 Created with Vellum

PART ONE

ONE

"ARE YOU SURE IT'LL WORK?"

"It'll work."

"He's late. He's not coming."

"He's not late."

Jon Bartlett would have rounded on his mates with exasperation ... if he'd had the room to do so.

Crammed into a maintenance compartment with the two other teens, though, made any movement difficult and awkward. There were already places touching that teenage boys generally didn't care to have such contact with their mates, no matter they'd spent some years at school together.

Well, he wouldn't truly mind a bit of awkward touching with Kaycie Overfield, but it would be a bit icky at the moment, what with Wyne in the compartment with them. Not to mention that she'd made it clear over the last two years that she didn't share the same desires.

It was hot and stuffy, as well as crowded, and none of that was helped by the fact that they were all wearing balaclavas over their heads in case they were seen.

Instead, he watched his tablet intently, double checking the connections to the maintenance panel and waiting for a figure to appear on the camera feed he'd hacked into.

"Are you certain it'll work?"

"Look, Wyne, I've tested it, haven't I?" He heard Kaycie start to speak. "Kaycie, I bloody swear, if you say he's not coming, I'll yank your bloody tongue right out of your mouth."

Jon counted off nearly thirty seconds of silence.

"He's late," Wyne whispered.

Jon closed his eyes and counted ten. Kaycie and Wyne were decent mates, the most decent he could hope to find at The Lesser Sibward Merchant Spacer Preparatory School, but there was no doubt they were a pair of whingers when it came to any sort of waiting.

No patience, either of them.

He opened his eyes to study his tablet again.

"*Hst!* There he comes."

A figure had appeared in the camera image. Jon checked the time on his tablet. It was two minutes of one in the afternoon, just when he'd predicted their target would be heading for the bog. "Just on time, too. Regular as a clock, that one."

"Regular as prunes," Wyne added, and Kaycie laughed out loud.

"*Ssh!*"

Jon silently noted the time, to the second, when their target went through the loo's hatchway.

"Do it!" Wyne whispered, voice harsh and tense.

"He's not there yet," Jon said, exercising as much patience as he could with his friends.

"How do you know?"

"I've timed it, right?" Jon said. "'Know your enemy. Learn everything you can about him. His habits, his loves, his hatreds, and his desires — then use all that to crush him.'"

"You reading that *Hso-Hsi* bloke again?" Kaycie asked.

"Chinese — precolonization," Jon said absently, watching the clock. "But, no, that's my father, said that."

"Holds a grudge, does he?"

"Nurses it like a baby at its mother's teat, he does."

Jon poised his finger over his tablet where he'd set the controls he'd hacked into. Most people didn't realize the degree of fine-grained control modern grav-plates allowed — over individual plates, even. It wasn't an all-or-nothing bargain. In fact, it wasn't only gravity, as most thought of it, that the plates could simulate.

"*Do it!*"

"Just a few seconds more ..."

Jon nodded as the clock passed his target time. No, not just gravity that pulled someone down, but they could also go negative. More than zero-g, they could actually repulse things and send the whole lot up. He touched the tablet's surface and slid his finger upward — not too quickly, he didn't want to injure their target, just ...

The three could hear the shrieks of outrage even from where they were in the maintenance compartment.

Jon slid the control all the way to the top, then eased it back down again. He stopped not quite at the control's bottom.

"*Go!*" he yelled, pulling the cables from his tablet and spinning to push the others to hurry them along.

Wyne slid the hatch open and the three of them spilled out into the corridor, stumbling and tripping over one another in their haste.

The shrieks were louder now, without the maintenance closet's closed hatch to muffle them.

They'd barely gained their footing when the hatch to the professors' loo slid open and the sounds of outrage filled the corridor.

Jon stared for a moment in slack-jawed awe as Professor Smallidge, bane of many a first-year's comparative economics grade, came into view.

His hair and clothing were wet, soaked with water and ... well, Professor Smallidge was well known for his digestive issues. Regular in timing, he might be, but that did nothing for the material in question.

"You boys! You there!" Smallidge started toward them, face red where it wasn't brown. "You did this, you little bastards! I'll —"

Smallidge's feet went out from under him, leaving disgusting brown streaks on the deck, and he landed prone on his back.

———

"'YOU DID THIS! You little bast — *urk*'" Wyne mimed his feet flying out from under him and flung himself prone on his bunk.

Kaycie collapsed on the other lower bunk, holding her stomach as she laughed.

Jon watched her roll on the bunk, entirely taken in by the sight. He frequently had to force down the thoughts her trim figure brought to mind, and remember that she wanted to be nothing more than mates with him. It was a bit of torture he often thought must be punishment for some vile sin he'd committed in a past life.

Despite the frustration it would bring, though, he often wished she berthed with him and Wyne, instead of their having to put up with Peavey and Scoggins. Scoggins was all right, he supposed, but Peavey was a right prat. Of course, Kaycie was only second year, while they were third, so that wasn't even an option.

Jon tossed his tablet onto his bunk, the one atop Wyne's, and smiled, but he didn't laugh out loud. He was busy replaying things in his mind, seeing where they'd gone wrong at the end.

"Should've left him at a tenth negative-g," he muttered. "Stuck up at the ceiling unless he pulled himself down and over to another grav-plate."

"Oh, give off, Jon!" Wyne sat up and wiped his eyes. "Then we'd never've seen him. No, with graduation two months away that was the perfect end to our time at good old Lesser Sewer. Oh, lord, the sight!"

"Oh, lord, the *smell!*" Kaycie cried out. "Got a whiff right down the corridor!"

"Still," Jon said, "he saw us."

"In balaclava?" Wyne asked. "And those down a trash chute already?"

Jon frowned. He'd turned off the corridor cameras along their route back to the rooms, all except the one just outside the loo so he could see Smallidge arrive, so there was no record of them fleeing, disposing of the balaclavas, or even leaving and returning to their room. So far as the cameras were concerned, the three of them had been in this room since just after breakfast. The other residents of the room, Thornton Peavey and York Scroggins, had morning classes, so wouldn't be able to say differently. He thought they were safe, despite being seen by Smallidge, but it still nagged at him.

His tablet *pinged* for his attention and he retrieved it from the bunk.

"Damn," he muttered at the sight of the message.

"What?" Wyne asked.

Jon frowned. "Summoned to headmaster."

Both Kaycie and Wyne grabbed their own tablets.

"Nothing for me."

"Me neither."

"I suppose he just assumes I was involved," Jon mused. If all three of them weren't summoned, then the headmaster was probably just fishing.

"There was poo involved," Kaycie said. "Small wonder you're the first one they think of."

"I don't —" Jon broke off. He supposed there was a bit of a scatological theme running through many of his pranks. He'd have to look into that and see about changing things up a bit.

Not good to be predictable.

He took a deep breath and slid his tablet into a pocket.

"Well, nothing for it but to face the Inquisition."

"We were all three right here studying," Wyne said.

"Surely," Kaycie agreed.

"MISTER BARTLETT. How good of you to come."

"Headmaster Fitt," Jon said, nodding.

He stood in front of the headmaster's desk, not taking one of the visitors' chairs — Fitt very rarely invited a student to sit.

Fitt was silent for a time, reading some document displayed on his desktop, then finally sat back in his chair and looked at Jon.

"Mister Bartlett," Fitt repeated.

Jon started to become worried. Fitt's face was as impassive as always, but there was a gleam in the man's eyes. Almost as though he were ... happy? No, that couldn't possibly be it. The headmaster was as dour an old stick as there ever was. Jon didn't think anyone had ever seen him smile. Still ... those eyes.

"You've heard about Professor Smallidge's mishap, I assume?" Fitt asked.

"Mishap?" Jon tried to keep his own face impassive, or at least displaying only the sort of mild curiosity one might expect at such a question when one was entirely innocent of the events.

"A gravitational fluctuation in the heads." Fitt leaned farther back in his chair, looking positively casual. "Just the sort of thing that's up your alley, I believe."

Jon forced a puzzled look to his face, then added a bit of concern.

"I'm sorry, sir, I haven't heard ... I do hope he's all right?"

The corners of Fitt's mouth turned up. Not quite a smile, but enough to send a chill through Jon.

Good lord, where'd I bollox it up? What didn't we think of?

"You have been a thorn in my side these many years, Mister Bartlett," Fitt said. "A pebble in my shoe. A pea under my mattress."

Pea under the mattress? An image of Fitt in princess-garb sprang to mind and Jon had to bite the inside of his cheek to keep from laughing. *Have to share that with Wyne and Kaycie.*

"Yes, you and your constant shadows, Mister Proffit and Miss Overfield. I'd thought Mister Peavey might provide an acceptable influence on you three, but he seems to have failed in that."

Knew the prat was reporting to you. Bloody wanker.

Fitt took a deep breath and now he did smile. Jon stared at him with a growing foreboding.

"And now I'm shut of you." Fitt leaned forward and slid his fingers over his desk. He turned the document he'd been reading to face Jon and slid it across the desk. "You won't have heard yet, of course. My condolences."

Puzzled, Jon bent to read.

It was a news report out of Greater Sibward and the headline made his knees buckle.

Bartlett Shipping Stock Plummets!
Notes called! Bonds questioned!

Jon vaguely felt himself come to rest in the headmaster's visitors' chair. He couldn't even bring himself to read the article, just the headline was enough. How could their notes have been called? The company was solid financially, his father wouldn't have it any other way, and the banks knew that. Their bonds were all held by the appropriate third-parties, their validity was unquestionable. What could have ...

"There's more, I'm afraid," Fitt said. "Been nearly six weeks since the last ship from Greater Sibward arrived in-system, you know. Plenty can happen in such a time." He reached across his desk and swiped the article away to be replaced by the next, then again and again, so rapidly that Jon could only take in the headlines, though that was more than enough.

Bartlett Shipping Scandal Worsens!
Were Bartlett ships used for smuggling?

Marchant Company to Guarantee Bartlett Bonds!

Frederick Marchant says: "The integrity of the transport system must not be put in question!"

Bartlett Allegations Worsen!

Stolen cargoes! "Piracy claims an inside job" says major insurer!

Criminal Charges Imminent in Bartlett Scandal!

Insurers to sue over false piracy claims!

Fitt jabbed his finger down on the latest article.

"Again, my condolences, Mister Bartlett."

He flicked his finger to the side.

Edward Bartlett Dead!

Apparent Suicide! Where will the blame fall now?

Jon felt his eyes burn and his throat tighten. His father was dead? Killed himself? Could he really have been involved in all that?

He didn't see how it could be true. His father was an honest man — hard, yes, and a ruthless businessman, but he was scrupulously honest.

Was.

My father is dead.

Fitt's finger jabbed the headline and flicked again.

Elizabeth Bartlett Pleads Guilty!

No further charges sought! "We are satisfied" says Crown Prosecution Service!

Jon felt his vision blur. Mother, too? And pled guilty so quickly?

Fitt was speaking, but Jon couldn't make out the words. There was a rushing noise in his head and the sides of his vision contracted until all he could see was the headline, then that blurred too and he knew nothing at all.

———

JON FELT HIS EYELIDS FLUTTER. He could hear voices, but not understand the words. He knew he was waking up, but didn't want to. He wanted to dive back down into the darkness. There was something in waking life he needed to avoid, but he couldn't recall what it was. The voices became clearer and he fought against hearing them — that way lay pain, something he wanted to avoid.

"Mister Bartlett! Wake up!"

Fitt.

The headmaster.

It all came back to him — the lark of pranking Professor Small-idge, followed by the call to Fitt's office and the revelation that ...

My father's dead. And ...

"Mother."

The word came unbidden from him.

"Transported," Fitt said, as though it had been a question, "for fraud, and indentured for debt. Though I doubt she or any of your family could hope to repay those you've cheated."

Jon opened his eyes. He was in the school's clinic. Fitt stood by the bed and Mistress Virden, the nurse, hovered behind him.

"The boy needs rest, headmaster," Virden said. She was frowning, brow furrowed.

"He can do that once I've finished with him," Fitt said.

"We cheated no one," Jon said. His voice sounded weak to his own ears.

"Your father killed himself for shame and your mother's admitted it!" Fitt was practically yelling now. "Up with you!"

He grasped Jon's shoulder and pulled him upright in the bed. Jon's head swam and his vision blurred again.

"You must leave him be, sir!" Virden stepped forward and reached out a hand to push Jon back down.

"You must mind your place, Mistress Virden," Fitt said. "This is none of your affair. I shouldn't have called for you when the boy fainted to begin with."

Virden stepped back and Fitt dragged Jon upright, twisting him so that he sat on the edge of the bed.

"I had Peavey pack your things for you," Fitt said, pointing to a spacer's travel bag next to the bed. "It's time for you to be on your way!"

"On my way?" Jon asked, confused. What did Fitt mean? Was he to go home? Was there even a home to go to with his father dead and mother transported?

"Away," Fitt said. "You've no place here any longer. This school is for proper merchant shippers, not ..." He scowled. "Not the spawn of criminals and cheats."

Jon stared at him. There was other family, but he wasn't sure he could rely on them or what their status was. Most worked the family's ships, with only a few, like his parents, resident on Greater Sibward.

Fitt was using this as an excuse to get rid of him, but the school might well be the only place Jon had right now. He narrowed his eyes, thinking.

"I've done nothing — nothing to be expelled for," he said. "My tuition's paid through term's end, isn't it?"

Fitt scowled. "Think you'll play the space lawyer with me, boy?" He grasped Jon's arm in a painful grip and dragged him to his feet. "We can expel any student who damages the school's reputation — which your family's certainly done. As for tuition, well, I'm sure a refund will be issued after a proper accounting's been made." He shook Jon. "I'll see it's sent right along to your family's creditors and victims."

He shoved Jon toward the hatchway.

"Now shoulder your bag and off with you!"

Jon thought to argue more. He looked to Virden, thinking she might help him, but she'd backed away and wouldn't meet his eye.

He picked up the bag. It was the same well-worn spacer's bag he'd arrived with at the beginning of the term. Students were allowed only the one bag, it was supposed to teach them to pack lightly for their future as officers aboard trading vessels. Jon often thought it was because limiting possessions was yet another way for the faculty to control the students.

He supposed the reason didn't really matter now — it simply meant that the bag would contain everything he had in the world. A few clothes, his vacsuit, his tablet, and personal mementos. If mother had pled guilty and been transported for debt, then all of their possessions — the house and offices on Greater Sibward, everything in it, and certainly the company assets themselves — would have been liquidated already.

How could it all happen so quickly?

"Move!" Fitt yelled.

Jon glared at him, but did as he was told, still in too much shock to think of how to protest more. Out of the clinic, past the administrative offices, and right up to the school's main hatchway. He saw no one at all and wondered if Fitt had ordered the way kept clear.

Fitt ushered him through the hatch and then slammed it shut behind him, uttering not another word.

———

JON STOOD STILL FOR A TIME, watching traffic in the station corridor pass back and forth before him.

He thought, perhaps, the hatch behind him might slide open again and Fitt or some other teacher might come out and tell him there'd been a terrible mistake, a tremendous misunderstanding, and he should come back in at once.

He'd never even been out in the main station alone before, only ever with other students on those rare occasions when some sort of holiday was granted. Lesser Sibward had not been chosen for the school's site because of any amenities it might have. In fact, quite the opposite was the case.

Lesser Sibward, as a star system, had little to offer other than raw ore to be had by the miners. There were no habitable planets at all and most of the station catered to those miners. The school was generally closed off from the rest of the station. Students could even arrive and depart from the private quays where the school's own ships docked. Those ships were used to teach the basics of sailing the Dark, as well as cargo handling and loading.

Jon had no doubt that, given only a few good hands to work the sails, he could manage one of those ships and make it to Greater Sibward in a week's time at most. He could hand, reef, and steer, himself. He was a decent navigator — not the best, perhaps, but then everyone struggled with *darkspace* navigation a bit. The idea that the distance traveled changed in relation to how close one's ship was to a normal-space mass took getting used to. He was even a competent gunner, given that the Lesser Sibward School's position on the matter was for merchants to strike one's colors and surrender at the first shot of a pirate, and then hope to be set adrift near a path with heavy traffic.

None of that, though, had prepared him to be cast adrift like this. Alone on a station with no friends, no resources, and only the few coins left in his pockets and accounts.

That brought to mind his finances, so he quickly checked his pockets and tablet. Twelve shillings and seven pence in his pockets, with only two pounds four shillings in his accounts. To be thorough, he tried to access the family accounts as well, but couldn't even view them. They'd likely been frozen by the courts and were long since emptied.

So ... two and sixteen, with a few pennies.

He wouldn't starve, not right away, at least, but neither was it enough to make any kind of start. He wasn't even sure how far it would get him on his journey home. He could estimate the cost of a cubic meter of cargo well enough, but Bartlett Shipping didn't ...

Hadn't. Damn me.

Bartlett Shipping hadn't done much in the way of passenger service. In fact, what few cabins might be available were most often left to the individual captains to set pricing on. Still, there was no telling until he'd asked.

First thing is to get home, see for myself what's happened and what's left.

That would mean a berth on a ship, preferably one going straight to Greater Sibward, even if there wasn't much traffic directly between the two systems. Most of Lesser Sibward's exports were raw ore, and that was taken to systems with refining and industrial bases. Greater Sibward was more business oriented and wanted finished goods more than raw ore.

Jon settled his bag more comfortably on his shoulder and looked around to get his bearings. A ship it would be, then.

The quayside was lined with them, but a quick check of the departures board showed only one going to Greater Sibward. Likely the same one just arrived from there, the one that the stories of his family's doom had arrived on. Regardless, that was the one he needed.

Jon made his way down the quay. He noted that most of the ships in-system were Marchant Company vessels, their distinctive logo of stylized blue waves in a red circle prominent on nearly every berth's display screen.

He reached the berth he was looking for and tapped the call screen beside the hatchway. It was only a moment before the call was answered, showing that the vessel kept a decent station-watch, at least.

"Yes?" a woman asked.

"I've come to inquire about passage to Greater Sibward," Jon said.

"A moment."

Jon waited and a short time later the hatch slid open and a woman in a ship's jumpsuit came out. She wore a third mate's insignia on her collar and looked Jon over with an appraising eye.

"Passage to Greater Sibward, you said?"

Jon nodded.

"Four pounds seven shillings."

Jon looked at her askance. That was almost twice the funds he had available.

"I was thinking, perhaps, more along the lines of one pound even," he said, "I've no need of luxury."

"Four and seven," the woman repeated. "I've one cabin left."

Jon's shoulders slumped. That was it then. He'd have to find some way to sustain himself until the next ship docked and see about passage then. Unless ...

"Are you taking on hands, by any chance?"

The woman frowned. "You?"

"I'm not a miner. I know my way around a ship."

The woman looked him over. "Ordinary spacer, one and twelve the month." She cocked her head. "Two-year contract."

That wouldn't work at all — he only needed to get to Greater Sibward and see about meeting any of the family who were still there. A two-year contract wasn't something he could commit to, nor would he want to — and he couldn't jump ship, as that would be something that would forever stain his records.

"I'm rated Able, at least, and could easily strike for master's mate," he said. He was trained, come to that, as a ship's officer, but they'd not hire an unknown for that. "I've trained at Lesser Sibward Merchant here."

The woman perked up at that. "Graduated?"

"Well, no, but —"

"Transcripts? Certificates?" The woman's voice was growing impatient.

Jon shook his head. The school would issue those closer to graduation, and likely not to him, even if he'd qualified for them.

"Ordinary. One and twelve the month. Two-year contract."

"Look, I'll work for free — only for my passage, please —"

"Four and seven for passage. One and twelve the month for hire. Two-year contract."

Jon longed to reach out and strangle the woman, but that wouldn't get him either berth. He met her eyes and thought he saw mockery there, but there was little he could do about it. Instead his shoulders slumped and he turned from her without a word.

"TUPPENCE."

Jon raised his eyes slowly from where he'd been examining the surface of the pub's table. The barmaid had set his fresh glass on the table and was staring at him impatiently. Head fuzzy with the drinks he'd already had, he gave her what he thought was a charming smile.

"Tuppence," the girl repeated.

Jon nodded. "Absolutely," he said.

He reached out for the small stack of coins on the table, his change from the single shilling he'd started with, all he'd allowed himself for the evening's wallowing in self-pity. He took one coin off the stack, placed it on the table top, and pressed his finger firmly atop it. Then he slid the coin toward the barmaid, left it at the edge of the table near her, and repeated the procedure with a second coin.

After four days of trying to find a ship, any ship, that might get him closer to Greater Sibward, he'd determined to get quite drunk.

I am quite drunk.

"Aye, y'are," the barmaid said. "Mind y'make no trouble."

Jon looked up at her blinking. "Did I say that aloud?"

The barmaid scooped the coins up and left, shaking her head.

Jon drained his previous glass and slid his new one into its place. He grimaced at the taste. A decent beer could be had for two pence the pint ... this was not a decent beer. It was a poor beer fortified with two generous shots of Blue Ruin, the vilest gin he'd ever tasted, but it was undeniably cheap and did its business quickly, which was what he was after.

It wasn't what he'd normally drink, but then nothing was normal anymore, was it?

He picked up the stack of coins he had left and slowly set them down in a new stack, one by one. Four coins. Two more drinks after he finished his latest.

"Three down, three to go," he muttered.

He grasped his latest and started to raise it to drink, but a hand fell on his forearm and pressed it to the table. A soft, feminine hand, which led, as he blearily moved his head to see — his eyes wouldn't seem to obey him — a similarly feminine forearm clad in a ship's jumpsuit of the Lesser Sibward School's colors. Higher to a slim shoulder with just a bit of dark hair falling over it. Jumpsuit's collar open just a bit to show a pale throat. He tilted his head back more to see ... it swung to the side a bit, as he was unable to control it so well, but he did manage to bring into view a set of bowed lips, pert button-nose, and almond eyes ever so slightly slanted.

"Kaycie?" He frowned. "It's late. School's locked up. You must be ... hall ... hallyou ..." He frowned more. "Bloody dream."

His drunken hallucination raised an eyebrow at him in amusement.

Well, if he was going to have drunken hallucinations, he couldn't think of a better one. He raised his head, waiting for its wobbling to align as best he could with hers, and leaned forward.

"Give us a kis — *ow!*"

His drunken hallucination had grasped his earlobe and pulled his head sharply back.

"You reek of gin and cheap beer."

Jon's brow furrowed. Could hallucinations smell?

"Kaycie?"

Kaycie shook her head and sighed. "Come on, then."

She took the beer from his hand and set it aside, then draped his arm over her shoulders. His other arm was grasped too, and he turned to find Wyne at his other side. Kaycie slid his remaining coins off the table and Wyne hefted his bag. The two rose, bringing Jon with them.

"There you go, mate," Wyne said. "One foot after the other — no, bloody *one* at a time, mind you!"

"I've three to go," Jon murmured.

JON WOKE IN A BUNK, which was quite a different experience than he'd had the last three mornings.

It is still only four, isn't it?

He had a sudden fear that he'd lost more than one night to drunkenness and quickly slid out of the bunk to find his tablet. That was a mistake as it set his head spinning and the small compartment he was in lurched and jumped about. He closed his eyes and sat still for a moment until his head and stomach settled. His bag was on the floor beside the bunk along with his jumpsuit. His tablet was still in the side pocket where he'd left it.

He sighed with relief as he checked it. Just the one night lost, though how he'd managed to wind up in a private compartment he didn't know. He'd spent the other nights wandering the shipping concourse and dozing in waiting areas. A private berth for the night cost more than he'd been willing to spend. He winced.

Must have done it drunk. I wonder how much it's cost me.

He frowned. His tablet showed a message waiting.

He'd received no messages from anyone at the school these last few days, so assumed they'd blocked his address in the school's system for either sending or receiving anything, and there hadn't been any ships docking from Greater Sibward that might have a message from his family.

He opened it.

You're paid there for three nights, so don't you bloody move or start to drinking again until we can get back out to you!
Wyne & Kaycie
PS — Bathe! K.

THAT BROUGHT BACK his memories of the night before. His decision to drink himself into a stupor, followed by Wyne and Kaycie showing up to drag him off.

The message made him wonder why he'd not received one before, though. They must have realized the school's systems were blocking things and sent from their private services.

Jon looked around the compartment. It wasn't grand, by any means, but it was certainly better than sleeping hunched over on a bench on the station's concourse. He wondered how they'd found him and felt a sudden warmth that they'd bothered. It was good to know there was still someone left who cared about him. A bit of the despair he'd begun to feel left him.

He reread the note and sniffed himself. Well, it had been four days since he'd left the school and no opportunity to bathe without using some of his limited funds — and then the drink last night, which seemed to have sweated out of him a bit.

He took the jumpsuits and underthings he'd worn into the shower with him and washed them as best he could, then hung them to dry.

The compartment air was chill on his bare skin, but he was loath to put on fresh clothing. He had only two laundered jumpsuits left in his bag and felt it was best to save them for when he might need to look his best when applying for a potential berth. Instead he wrapped himself in a sheet and settled onto the bunk with his tablet.

That quickly palled, though. There were no new ships in port that he could apply to and no more news from Greater Sibward about his family. No messages. Nothing.

He set the tablet aside and slept for a time.

His clothes were dry when he woke, so he dressed and exited the compartment.

The berth was one of a half dozen at the back of a small pub and opened into a short corridor that led to the common room. It was early and there were only two patrons, both spacers by their dress. A woman looked up from the bar as he entered.

"Sooner than I expected," she said, looking him over. "And not too worse the wear for your troubles last night."

Jon took a stool at the bar and grinned sheepishly. He must have looked a state being dragged in by Wyne and Kaycie the night before.

"Yes, but a bit at a loss ..."

The barkeep nodded. "Your friends left instructions for me. You're paid for three nights, meals included. But no drink," she warned with a stern look, "and I'm not to serve you even if you pull out your own coin."

Jon bridled at that. It wasn't as though he were a complete drunkard, and a moment's excess could be excused, given his situation, couldn't it? Still it was quite kind of Kaycie and Wyne to set him up like this.

"Food?" she asked.

Jon nodded. His stomach gave a little lurch.

"Something easy," he said.

She nodded and tapped the screen before her, then went through a door behind the bar. She returned a few moments later with a plate of fruit and dry toast.

"See how that sets, lad, and there'll be more if you like."

Jon nodded his thanks and set to slowly eating.

That and more stayed down and did make him feel a bit more human. He spent some time at the bar, drinking cold tea and pondering his circumstances, then moved back to his room as the pub began to fill.

It wasn't until late on the third evening that Wyne and Kaycie arrived. Jon had begun despairing that they would, as there'd been no further messages from them.

The three went back to his compartment. Wyne took the single chair and Jon sat cross-legged on the bunk. Kaycie joined him there, her knees almost touching his.

"How are you getting out of the school so late?" Jon asked.

Wyne grinned broadly. "I poached a professor's hatch code."

"Which one?" Jon was a bit in awe. That code would allow them to enter and leave the school compartments at will — any time of day or night. Such a code would have been the holy grail of his time at Lesser Sibward and now he was missing it.

"Might be that Smallidge left his office and computers unlocked when he was in such a hurry to reach the loo ... and hasn't been back to them since. Something about a leave of absence ..."

Jon laughed, then sobered. He looked at his two friends.

"Thank you. Both of you."

Kaycie patted his leg, which he almost wished she wouldn't do, since her touch felt like it set him on fire. He shifted uncomfortably.

"We tried to message you," she said, "and didn't know what to think when you didn't respond. Then Wyne reasoned out that the school was blocking your address in the systems. He thought to check Smallidge's office, which got us the code, and we came looking for you." She frowned. "Had a time of it finding you."

"So, we're here to help now," Wyne said. "What's the plan?"

Jon looked at them, confused. "Plan?"

"Surely you have a plan?" Kaycie said.

"I suppose I'll keep trying to find a berth aboard some ship," Jon said. "At first I thought to take passage to Greater Sibward, but hadn't the coin for it. They wouldn't accept me as crew on so short a run — wanted a longer contract. By the time I was desperate enough for anything, that ship had sailed, though." He looked down at where his fingers were picking at the sheet between his legs.

Kaycie caught his hands in hers and shook them.

"No, Jon, your *plan*."

He looked up and met her eyes. She seemed to be expecting something of him, but he couldn't imagine what. How was he to plan anything other than to accept the first berth that would take him? He had no funds to speak of. Wyne and Kaycie would have a bit of their allowances, but not enough to keep him for long and he wouldn't ask it of them. He'd had no word of his family and no way to contact them. What plan?

Kaycie squeezed his hands again and gave him a little smile.

"You always have a plan, Jon. Every bit of mischief we've been about these last two years has come from you."

She glanced over at Wyne who nodded at him.

"What do you need and how can you go about getting it?" she asked. "Surely the great Jon Bartlett is not prepared to admit the universe is cleverer than him?"

Jon looked away. She was expecting too much of him. Pranking a teacher was one thing, but for this ... for this, even leaving aside the cost, he needed a ship to be bound for Greater Sibward and there were none in port. He started to say so — to tell her it was easy enough for her to say that, when all she had to do tonight was slip back into the school and then slip back into her bunk and wake to her life that hadn't been upended as his had been.

He paused.

Slip back into the school. The Lesser Sibward Merchant *Spacer* Preparatory School. The one that taught them how to sail the Dark between star systems, along with all the bits about cargo and finances. He needed a ship.

He caught her eye, surprised at the real concern he saw there. For a moment, he thought it might be something more, but then the corner of her mouth quirked up and she grinned.

"That's the look of my Jon," she said. "You've got something now. What's the plan?"

"BLOODY MADNESS," Wyne muttered.

Jon had his tablet out as they marched boldly through the school corridors. This late at night there was no one roaming the halls and the prefects relied on the cameras and motion sensors to alert them. Wyne's and Kaycie's codes let them into the school and Jon's tablet was still able to control the cameras. The headmaster might have locked him out of the school's messaging system, but no one had known he'd hacked his tablet into a dozen others over the years. They'd only shut him out of the systems he'd had legitimate access to.

"They'll hang us, you know?" Wyne muttered again.

"Put a stopper in it, Wyne," Kaycie whispered.

"It's *piracy!*"

"It's not," Jon said. "I looked it up. It's only piracy if the ship's crewed and a-space. This is simple theft. Hijacking at the worst."

"Simple theft of a whole bloody skiff," Wyne said. "What's the value? Three hundred pounds? We'll be transported for sure!"

"It's only me on the hook, really," Jon said. "They'll never even know you two were with me once I sail it away."

Wyne shook his head. "You'll never make it. It's a week's sail to Greater Sibward — and that's in a proper ship. Two weeks in a skiff and skiffs aren't even supposed to leave a system, you know that!" He skipped ahead of Jon and Kaycie and turned to face them, walking backward. "You'll miss it all entire, go Dutchman, and be lost in the Dark."

"Wyne," Kaycie said, "this is what Jon needs to do and I'm helping him. You either help along with me or bugger off, but either way put a bloody sock in it, will you?"

"I'm just saying —"

"Well, stop saying." Kaycie ran her hand over Jon's back. He'd noticed she was touching him a great deal — not that he minded at all, it was simply confusing him. "He needs our help, not your naysaying. Now are you in or out?"

"In," Wyne grumbled, but turned to walk with them.

They made one stop at the school's galley, loading a second bag with supplies for his journey, then made their way to where the skiffs were docked. The school's private quay was every bit as deserted as the rest of the corridors. The half dozen hatches lining the outside of the corridor were all closed, but the viewports next to each were clear, showing the craft docked there. He'd honestly prefer to take one of the larger craft on such a long journey, but they'd be too hard to crew alone. A skiff could be crewed by one and should be able to make the trip. He had food enough, so long as he didn't — as Wyne seemed convinced — miss Greater Sibward all entire.

Jon checked his tablet once more. Everything was as it should be, sending out the signal so that the corridor and hatch sensors saw nothing, heard nothing, and, most importantly, reported nothing. He chose a hatch at random. All of the skiffs were the same.

He set his bag down and examined the dock's hatch. He'd never actually worked with any of the airlock hatches before and wanted to make sure there wasn't something different about it.

"Did you hear that?" Wyne whispered.

Jon listened for a moment. Wyne was probably just being a paranoid again. Then he heard it too, a soft *tap*, as of someone trying to walk stealthily and putting one step down a bit too hard on the deck.

"Bloody —"

He looked around to find somewhere they could hide, but it was too late.

"Ha!"

Thornton Peavey, Jon and Wyne's roommate, rounded the corner and caught sight of them. He pointed at them, a wide, satisfied grin on his face.

"I *knew* it! Knew you were up to something, Wyne!" He pointed at Jon. "And you're expelled! When the headmaster finds out you broke in you'll be lucky not to face charges!"

"Peavey, shut up!" Wyne said.

Peavey stalked up to them.

"Oh, no," he said. "I want to enjoy this moment, I do."

Jon's stomach felt like it was filled with lead. It was all over. Even if he could get onto the skiff and away now, he'd never make it out of the system. Peavey would alert the headmaster and they'd send a station patrol boat after him. He'd likely not even make it to a transition point.

"Look, Peavey," he said. "I made them help me, right? Just let Wyne and Kaycie go and I'll come with you to the headmaster."

He likely would face charges, though breaking into the school was less to be caught at than if he'd managed to undock the skiff before being found out.

Thankful for small things, I suppose.

"What? And give up seeing all three of you be expelled?" Peavey grinned. "No chance of that."

Kaycie had been oddly quiet since Peavey arrived, she usually was when he was around for some reason, but now she gave Jon a strange look and seemed to straighten her shoulders. He could see the corners of her jaw tighten, as though she'd found some inner resolve. She stepped up to Peavey.

"What, little miss? You have something to —"

Jon and Wyne gasped in shock, but not as loudly as Peavey did as Kaycie drove her knee up into his fork.

Peavey doubled over, knees bent and clutching himself. Strange, strangled sounds emerged from his mouth, but he seemed to be having a great deal of trouble breathing.

Kaycie bent close to his head and whispered so low that Jon wasn't sure he heard correctly.

"Do you remember my first year, Peavey? Well I'm no longer a scared girl just away from home for the first time. You bugger off and keep your mouth shut, or the headmaster'll hear about more than this business, you hear me?"

"You ... ruddy ... bitch ..." Peavey rasped.

"I can't quite hear you," Kaycie said. She grasped his shoulders to help him stand. "Here, straighten up a bit. It'll help you breathe."

"Bloody ... *bitch* ..."

"That's what I thought it was."

Kaycie took a step back, then swung her foot up hard. Peavey made a croaking sound, his eyes bulged, and he toppled to the floor.

She bent and whispered to Peavey again, but Jon couldn't hear this time. He shared a look with Wyne who seemed as shocked and puzzled as he was.

"Right, then," she said, turning to them. "Jon, you get the lock open. Wyne, you wait out here and see Peavey doesn't cause more trouble. I'll see Jon in."

"Aye, aye," Wyne said, seemingly without realizing it.

Jon raised an eyebrow, but turned back to the hatch's lock.

It seemed to have nothing special about it and soon yielded to his tablet. It slid open and he shouldered his bag. Kaycie hefted the bag of food and followed him in.

"What was that about?" he asked as the station-side hatch closed and they waited for the skiff's hatch to cycle. "What'd he do your first year?"

Kaycie flushed and looked down at the deck. "You heard that? Bugger."

They entered the skiff. It was a small craft and had only one compartment. The fusion plant and engineering controls were at the rear. A navigation plot with integrated signals took up most of the space in the center and there was a small galley along one bulkhead with two bunks along the other.

Jon had a moment's apprehension. A craft this size was meant for intrasystem sails. A few days in *darkspace* at most and never away from where its optics could pick up the lights of a pilot boat or beacon. The two-week sail to Greater Sibward was quite another matter. He'd be wholly reliant on his own skills as a navigator to not miss the target system entirely. Moreover, he'd be spending most of that time in his vacsuit, as he'd have to move in and out of the ship to adjust the sail.

He tossed his bag toward the bunk and started checking the engineering systems. Kaycie set the bag of food near the galley and joined him.

"So?" he asked.

Kaycie sighed. "It's nothing really."

"Not nothing if it warrants a blow like that to the bollocks, it seems to me."

"It's nothing. He cornered me in the corridor outside the gymnasium my first week." She sighed again. "A bit of a grope — nothing to it, really."

"Bastard!"

Kaycie stiffened. "And there it is. Thank you for your outrage on my behalf, but I've no need of it."

"I only meant —"

"Know what you meant."

The engineering systems were online and she turned from him to check the navigation plot.

He stared at her back for a moment.

"Why didn't you go to the headmaster then and get him expelled?"

Kaycie snorted. "Really? There's a chance of that, I suppose, but his family's far wealthier than mine. He's, what, sixth generation Lesser Sewer? Headmaster'd believe us over him? And then, of course, everyone would know."

"Us?"

She left off the navigation plot and went to the galley area, starting to unpack his supplies. "I know of two other girls — one went further. We try to warn the first years about him." She turned to him with a wan smile. "Bit of a club, really."

Jon hesitated, uncertain what to do. He wanted to wrap her up in his arms and tell her it would be all right — at the same time he wanted to rush back into the corridor and pound Peavey's face into the deck.

"Kaycie —"

"And there it is, see? It's either that look and that tone, 'Oh, poor you, it'll be all right, let me make it better.' Or the other, that we're not believed and must've done something to lead the poor bloke on.

That's why we don't say anything, isn't it? It's never the same after someone hears — can't be just Jon and Kaycie —"

She broke off and scrubbed at her eyes.

Jon stood still, afraid to move.

"Damn him for showing up," Kaycie said. "This isn't how this bit was supposed to go." She walked up to Jon and pulled something from her pocket with a wan grin. "Look, I made you something to see you off." She reached up and slipped a bit of black cloth around his head, blocking one of his eyes with it. "Proper pirate, right?"

"I told you, it's only common thef —"

He broke off, eyes wide, as she grasped his face and kissed him. Then he closed his eyes and fell into the kiss, which was really quite good, he thought, even given his limited experience for comparison. Better than the kiss, even, was the feel of her body against his, and as soon as the shock wore off he reached to wrap his arms around her and make that even better.

But before he could, the kiss ended. Kaycie released his face and dashed past him to the hatch, sliding it open and calling back, "I expect to see you again, Jon Bartlett."

Jon stared at the closed hatch for a long moment, then reached up and pulled the eyepatch from his head. He raised a finger to his lips, which still seemed to feel the press of hers. He shook his head slowly.

"I will never in life understand girls."

"YOU LOOK A FRIGHT, lad, have you eaten?"

Jon took his Uncle Wyatt's offered hand. He supposed he did look frightful.

He'd arrived at Greater Sibward without incident and docked the skiff at the public quay. It would be investigated once it was seen to have been docked there past the time limit and someone would contact the school to see about its return.

Since then, though, things had gone poorly.

29

It seemed as though the family had scattered, disappearing from both the station and planet, and even long time employees and associates neglected to return his calls and messages.

He'd sold his better clothes and other things for a few coins to keep him going just a bit longer. He was down to under a pound, all told, and despairing that he'd find work or a way off Greater Sibward. Light as his pack was now, with just a single change of clothes, vacsuit, and his tablet, he'd likely have to sell those as well soon. It seemed that any time a ship's master learned his name, there were suddenly no positions available.

It had been with some relief that he'd finally received a response from one of his many messages to family members. Uncle Wyatt was still in-system, but not in the home Jon remembered. To Jon's relief he'd responded and agreed to meet, but the expression on his uncle's face didn't allow that relief to last long.

Uncle Wyatt took his arm and steered him down the corridor.

"There's a pie shop around the corner. You need to eat."

They got their pies at the counter, Wyatt insisted Jon get two, found seating, then sat with only the sounds of their eating until Jon had finished.

"I'm so sorry, lad, I can't begin to say."

"Uncle Wyatt ..." Jon thought he had a million questions, but suddenly found that they call came down to one. "What happened?"

Wyatt winced.

"I tried to get a message to you, lad, I did. But by the time it reached your school you'd already gone."

"They threw me out as soon as word came."

Wyatt winced again.

"Why didn't anyone send for me earlier?"

"You have to understand, Jon, it was eight weeks of hell. That's all it took, you see, start to finish. Five generations to build and eight bloody weeks to end us." He sighed. "By the time we saw how bad it was, we went to bed every night exhausted from fighting it and woke up the next morning to find it worse than before. You were safe at school, we thought ..."

"What happened?" Jon repeated.

"It was so damned quick," Wyatt said. He toyed with his fork, pushing a bit of crust around his plate, making trails through the gravy. Jon started to ask again, but then simply waited. He could tell it was hard for his uncle and he'd get the story in good time.

"At first it was the stock," Wyatt said finally. "Blocks were being sold off, more than usual, and the price started falling. Not much at first, just a bit. We, your parents and I, found it odd — profits were up, we'd just sent a dividend. The company was strong.

"Then it was more than blocks being sold, there were short sales — someone without the stock selling at a lower price than it was listed. That made no sense, for they were always so far below the market that ... someone would have to buy at a higher price to sell at the lower. It was madness, but it drove the price of the stock down further.

"Edward, your father, bought some, to keep the price up ... we all did, really. Everyone in the family, we bought and bought. And with company funds, too. Why not? The shares were far below their value by that time and we knew Bartlett Shipping was strong. But it kept going, down and down, and we didn't have enough ready cash to buy more shares."

Wyatt looked up and his eyes were haunted.

"Loans?"

"Aye, loans." Wyatt nodded. "Company lines of credit, personal, whatever it took. And still there was always someone offering shares at a lower price than the market. Not just a bit lower, but ... so low it looked like ..."

Jon realized what it must have looked like. Why would someone offer to sell at a lower price than the market offered, unless they felt they needed to get rid of the stock quickly?

"Like someone in the know. Who'd sell so low, but someone who knew a secret about the company ..."

Wyatt nodded again. "Aye. And so everyone came to believe there must be a secret about the company. Got so our bank wouldn't talk to us, so we went to another and there were more loans, until near everything that could be an asset was tied up." He snorted. "Put our boots up as collateral, if they'd have let us. And why not? The shares were a bargain ..." He gave Jon a wry grin. "And the company was strong, aye?"

He sighed.

"Then came the rumors and the stories. Said we were smugglers at first." His jaw clenched as well as his fists and Jon could see how angry he was. "And that we'd pirated our own ships for the insurance."

"Father would never —"

"I know. None of us would, but especially not Edward. My brother was a right bastard, but he was a right-honest bastard."

Jon said nothing. It was the sort of characterization his father would hear and shrug, accepting the truth of it.

"The insurance company announced they'd investigate. What else could they do? But that drove things lower yet."

Wyatt looked around.

"Should've gone to a pub. I could use a stiff one." He rubbed his face with both hands.

"Then the Crown Prosecutor got involved. Not the man here, mind you, but a special one in from Bowstable. Just showed up one day. He had evidence, he said. Statements from men who were a part of it — taking our own ships and selling them and the cargoes, then making the insurance claims. And more statements that we were smuggling far and wide.

"That's what broke him. Edward. Your father." Wyatt's eyes were wet and red-rimmed when he looked up. "He used a laser. It was quick."

He reached across the table and squeezed Jon's hand, but Jon barely felt it.

"He left a note — said the prosecutor implied the whole mess would go away if somehow Edward wasn't about anymore. I don't know how that could be. But if a man knew your father he'd know that would be the way ... the way to make him do such a thing. 'Course it didn't go away.

"So, they turned those statements on Elizabeth, and I know for a fact what they said to her. 'Plead guilty,' they said, 'and we'll not go after the others in the family — the others named in the statements.'"

He looked up and met Jon's eyes again.

"You were named."

"Me?" Jon was shocked. He'd sailed aboard family ships, of course, even worked them, but what could he have been accused of?

"Statements made about your summer cruises. That you smuggled more than once on them. Not just what would avoid duty and tax, neither, but other things."

"I —"

"We know it's not true, Jon. Even if you were the sort to do it, what was described ... well, it would have taken others to be involved. Too many others."

"Then how could they have these statements?" Jon was confused. He hadn't understood how all of this could have happened, but it was sounding so much more bizarre than what he'd read.

Wyatt's eyes narrowed. "Do you not see it, Jon? Do you even yet think this was some misunderstanding or an accident? Just bad luck?"

"I don't know what to think. What —"

"In the end, the rest of the family had to give up their shares or join your mother in the dock, that was the other part of the deal. So, we lost the company — the whole of it gone in one swoop. And who do you think came in at the end? Buys the ships, the routes, reassures the shareholders who're left?"

Jon stared at him blankly, then frowned. That was no proof. Someone would have to buy the remnants, after all. "That doesn't prove —"

"The same being based on Bowstable where the Crown Prosecutor came from? The same who has holdings in the new bank we went to? The very bank that called our loans first? The same who had cause to wish your father harm for speaking against him in the guild and who has pockets deep enough to sell our stock short like it was water on Penduli?"

"Marchant ..." Jon couldn't believe it. True, his father had spoken against them and their ways more than once, but this?

"Frederick bloody Marchant and his Marchant Company," Wyatt said. He pulled his tablet from his pocket and slid it across the table to Jon. "Our solicitor managed one thing before it all fell apart. He got the statements made against us ... and the names of those making them. Small matter then to find out where those speakers are employed now."

Jon ran his eyes down the list. Nearly every name listed had an employer of the Marchant Company or one of its subsidiaries. More, he recognized many of the names. Men and women who'd worked for Bartlett Shipping and had worked with Jon himself on summer cruises. Of the names he recognized, there were none he'd have named good spacers or reliable hands — hard men and women, quick to anger and quicker to cause trouble aboard ship.

"But if we know this —"

"Knowing and proving are different things, lad."

"But —"

"And solicitors cost." Wyatt lowered his eyes. "There's none of us left with much. Not nearly enough." He shook his head. "All the assets were seized and orders went out to impound our ships in port. The family's scattered, penniless save what coin they have with them. I'm —" He cleared his throat. "Mary had a bit tucked away. In her name, from her family. It's not much, but it's enough for us and the little ones to get away from here. Buy a single share in some colony far out where they've never heard of what happened and the name Bartlett doesn't make people's noses wrinkle at the stench."

Jon's body was chilled. He couldn't believe what he'd heard. What he'd thought had happened was bad, he knew, but to hear that it had been done deliberately — not just happenstance ...

Frederick Marchant did this?

Caused it all. The family's ruin, his mother transported God knew where, his father's suicide ...

No, not suicide at all. It was murder, pure and simple, atop all the rest.

"You could come with us, lad," Wyatt said.

"What?" Jon looked up. He hadn't really heard. He'd been too lost in his thoughts and the sudden realization.

"Come with us. Mary and me." He shrugged. "Colonies're a hard life, I know, but ... it's better than what's left for you here, lad."

"Do you know where mother is?" She was all he had left, really. Perhaps that's where he belonged, helping her.

Wyatt shook his head. "Put aboard the transport ships and sent to the Fringe. No telling where her indenture was bought, unless she manages to get a message to someone."

Jon nodded. So that was out then. It would take far more time and coin to gain access to those records and travel to her than he had. The indenture ships traveled long loops amongst the Fringe Worlds, taking on and selling off indentures. It could be a year or more before that ship's records made it back to a central office — assuming, even, that it wasn't an independent ship that had no office more than its captain's cabin.

Mother's as much gone to me as father is.

"Come with us," Wyatt repeated. "A new world. A fresh start."

Jon stared at him for a moment. A fresh start ... it was really giving up, though, wasn't it? Fleeing and letting Marchant get away with it.

"Thank you for the offer, Uncle Wyatt, but I think there's ... I think there's more I need to do."

Wyatt shook his head.

"Oh, Jon, don't be a fool. Do you think I don't want vengeance myself? What do you think you'll do? Get yourself killed or jailed storming onto one of their ships with your pistol waving in the air?"

Jon shook his head.

"No. Father always counseled patience. I don't know just yet what I'll do, but I can't simply leave."

Wyatt met Jon's eyes for a long time, then his eyes filled and his lips trembled. Jon was shocked — he'd never seen his uncle in such a state.

"You've got his look about you," Wyatt said.

"What?"

"Edward's. That set of his jaw and the coldness in his eyes when he was hell and determined on something." He looked down at the table as though unable to meet Jon's eye. "I can't Jon. I have Mary and the little ones to think of ... I can't."

"I know, Uncle Wyatt. You and the others have families to care for — there's no one looking to me."

Wyatt pulled out his tablet. "I can give you a bit ... not much ... colony shares're dear."

"It's all right. You don't have to —"

"No. A hundred pounds, though I can't do more. Enough for a start." He looked up from his tablet. "You can't be a Bartlett, you know?"

"What do you mean?"

"The name, Jon. It's sullied now."

Jon nodded. He hadn't thought of that, but he'd experienced it with the hatches being shut on him as soon as he gave his name and documents.

"And then there's the Marchants. Frederick Marchant isn't known for doing things by half. He may not be done with us, at least if there's any of our name underfoot. That's why the family's scattered so far."

Jon frowned.

"There are men," Wyatt said, "who can forge what you need. You've heard of it, sure?"

He had. Some men would jump ship and seek out a new identity. He didn't know how to go about it though. How did one even begin?

"I've a couple places you can post messages," Wyatt said. "No names, but I've heard things. Don't go for the cheapest — not what the common hands would be able to pay. They'll not have work that'll hold up for long."

Jon nodded. His tablet *pinged* announcing the transfer of funds and messages from Wyatt.

Wyatt reached across the table and gripped his hand.

"If you're determined, well, then my best to you, lad. You get them, Jon. You get the bastards that did this to us and make them pay."

JON ENTERED the pub and headed straight for the bar. The messages he'd received in response to his veiled inquiries had mostly been dismissed, but one seemed promising. He couldn't be certain, of course. Aside from the illegality of it, there was the concern, as Uncle Wyatt had said, that the Marchants were not entirely done with the Bartletts.

The message had stated which table to go to, but Jon wanted to view the man he was to meet before going over.

"A pint of pils, if you please," he told the barkeep. "I'm not particular."

In fact, he planned to nurse the one drink through this entire meeting. He wanted his wits about him even after, in case it was a trap of some sort.

"Three," the barkeep said, sliding a glass in front of him.

Jon slid the coins back in return, wincing at the cost. Even with the hundred pounds from Uncle Wyatt, he begrudged every pence, as there was no telling when he'd be able to earn more. He raised his glass and took a sip, grimacing.

I should have been particular.

He set the glass down and used the mirror behind the bar to scan the compartment. The table he'd been instructed to go to was occupied by a single man. As Jon's gaze passed over him, the man looked up and met Jon's eyes in the mirror.

"Mister Bartlett!" he called out.

Jon jumped, startled. He hadn't mentioned his name in the messages and even if he had how would the man recognize him?

"Yoohoo!" The man waved a hand in the air. "Mister Bartlett! Over here! You seem to have forgotten which table I said!"

Jon looked around, but none of the other patrons seemed to be paying any attention. He hurried over to the table and sat down.

"Are you mad?" Jon glared at the man. He was tempted to leave, but this was the only response he'd received to his inquiry that seemed it might be valid. "Do you not understand the need for discretion?"

The man laughed. Now that he was viewing him up close, Jon tried to fix the man's appearance in his mind, but found there was simply nothing at all distinctive about him. Average, in every way, was the best he could come up with to describe him. Even his age was difficult to estimate — one moment Jon would swear the man was his own age and in the next, as though with a change of the light, he could be a decade or more older.

"Discretion? Whatever for?"

"This transaction," Jon whispered. He wished the man would lower his voice.

"Yes, well, I wouldn't have chosen a place where anyone would care what our business was, now would I?"

Jon looked around. True, no one seemed to be paying them the least bit of attention. Rather studiously so, given the man's volume.

"Who are you?"

"Ah, yes, the introductions." The man held out his hand. "Malcom Eades, at your service, Mister Bartlett. I represent ... well, let us say an organization to whom I believe you may be of some service in return for my being of service to you in this matter."

"And how do you know who I am? Or what service I might be?"

"It's my business to know things," Eades said. He signaled for the barkeep and ordered a bottle of wine, which was quickly delivered. Eades poured himself a glass and drank. He appeared to be in no particular hurry to discuss their business.

"Can you do it?" Jon asked finally.

"Do it?"

"Yes, damn you, the whole bit we discussed!"

Eades raised his eyebrows and took another sip.

"The whole bit, eh? A new identity, ship's officer certificates ... a past that doesn't haunt you, yes?"

Jon clenched his jaw. Who was this man to speak so to him? What did he know of a haunted past? He'd expected this to be a simple transaction, cash for the necessary work, not a bloody discussion of his life.

"Yes."

"No."

"No?"

Eades frowned. "Well, I suppose I could ... except the past bit, that would be on you, I'm afraid, but an identity and certificates I could accomplish if I chose to."

Jon stared at him for a moment, not at all certain he'd heard correctly.

"If you choose to? If you won't do it, why message me? Why meet?"

He scanned the room again, wondering if it was some trap of the Marchants and he should prepare to run.

"To convince you to change your plan, Mister Bartlett," Eades said. "Your current course is doomed to failure."

"You can't know what I plan. You're —"

Eades sighed. "Mister Bartlett, you wish a new identity and credentials as a ship's officer. You plan to find a berth with the Marchant Company, learn what you may of them and their ways, then cause them some harm in vengeance for what the Marchants did to your own family. Have I got it right? Left anything out?"

Jon stared at him in shock. He knew not only what Jon did,

indeed, plan, but so casually stated what no one else believed — that the Marchants were responsible for the harm done to the Bartletts.

"It is my business to know." Eades settled back into his chair and regarded Jon critically. "Your plan is unworkable on its face. Go aboard a Marchant ship as an officer, regardless of how well made your new documents are, and you'll be found out within a fortnight. The community of ship's officers is far too small — remarkably small and close, given the size of the universe and number of ships. Incestuous, even, it sometimes seems."

Eades took Jon's glass of beer, poured the contents onto the floor, seemingly without a thought that the proprietor might object, and then filled it halfway with wine from his bottle.

"Here. Have a proper drink. You look as though you could use one and that particular pilsner is vile."

Jon lifted the glass and drained it without really tasting the wine. It might as well have been the beer, vile as it was, for all he noticed. Eades filled the glass again when Jon lowered it.

"No," Eades continued. "You'll want to join the common crew, perhaps work your way to master's mate, but no higher. No more visibility than that." He filled his own glass and signaled for another bottle, waiting to speak more until it arrived. "Besides which, it's the crews that really knows things — where the bodies are buried, so to speak ... or possibly more literally than you imagine. The crews know and the crews have loose tongues — but not to an officer."

"Who are you?"

Eades smiled, the first thing Jon found remarkable about the man, and he felt a shiver run down his back. He decided he much preferred this man, Eades, as innocuous and unremarkable, rather than that distinctive smile.

"I am someone with whom your own interests coincide at this particular juncture, Mister Bartlett. You wish to know more about the Marchant Company." Eades shrugged. "I wish to know more about the Marchant Company. Why should we not assist each other in this mutual endeavor?"

Jon swallowed, throat tight. He was becoming more and more uneasy about Malcom Eades and began to wish he'd never posted his inquiry.

"The enemy of my enemy is my friend?"

"The enemy of your enemy is sometimes a useful tool, Mister Bartlett, it would be foolish not to make use of him." Eades smiled again. "I have no friends, I assure you.

"A new name, Mister Bartlett, untainted by scandal." He frowned, examining Jon. "Records of ... three years aboard ships, I think, so we'll make you a year or two older than you are. You can pass for that. Rated Able ... a brief stint as master's mate aboard your last ship, one that's now gone off far from the Sibwards, Lesser and Greater both, and away from any Marchant trading routes."

"Solid records?" Jon asked. "You can do that?"

"Solid as rock, Mister Bartlett." Eades smiled again, as though at some secret joke he found most amusing. "Solid as though Her Majesty Herself had stamped them for you."

"And in return?"

"You tell me what you learn. Simple as that." Eades held out his hand. "A bargain, sir?"

Jon eyed the hand for a moment. It was a deal with the devil himself, he suspected, but Eades was likely his only chance. No one else had responded to the message — it was as though no one had even seen it after Eades replied. Was vengeance worth it?

More than sup with the devil, I'd bend over for Lucifer himself if it would harm the Marchants.

He took Eades' hand.

"I expect it'll be neither simple nor a bargain, Mister Eades, but it is a deal."

JON CLENCHED his jaw and resisted the urges that were running through him.

This section of the Greater Sibward quay had been his family's docks, he'd grown up running through them, dodging crates and men as they loaded and unloaded ships. The logo of Bartlett Shipping had graced a dozen docking hatches here.

Now it was all Marchant.

"Watch yerself!" a stevedore yelled and Jon skipped aside to allow the man's load to pass.

The move put him next to one of the docks, its hatch screen bright with the Marchant logo. Jon stared at it for a moment, thinking about all he'd lost. His father, his mother, every member of his family scattered to far systems, and everything they'd worked for, five generations of Bartletts ... gone. Gone to Marchant, the men who'd engineered his woes to begin with.

It wasn't right that they should win. It wasn't right that they should profit.

They needed to pay.

He forced his fist to unclench so that he wouldn't punch the screen before him. His father's voice echoed in his mind.

Patience.

Know your enemy. Learn everything you can about him. His habits, his loves, his hatreds, and his desires — then use all that to crush him.

He knew what Marchant loved. Their ships, their cargoes, the money that came from them.

He'd learn as much as he could about the company, pass what he thought best on to Eades — perhaps the man was serious about harming Marchant as well, perhaps not. Either way he'd use Eades as well as he could.

And when I know it all, I'll crush them. Destroy them as they did us, father. I'll see they pay.

There was a recruiting table set up a few hatches down and another three docks after that. Some new Marchant ships, it seemed, had need of more hands, and that worked to Jon's purpose. He approached the first table, struggling to keep a charming, friendly smile on his face and show none of his true feelings.

"Looking for a berth?" the man behind the table asked.

Jon nodded and scanned the woman's rank tabs and then the docking information.

Second mate on ... the Elizabeth.

A former Bartlett ship they'd taken with the rest of the company and not bothered to rename.

The very ship my father named for mother.

All of the Bartlett ships had been named for the wives and daughters of the family. A five-generation tradition, fouled by the Marchants.

Jon clenched his jaw tightly, shook his head, and moved on. He couldn't stand to sail on a former Bartlett ship, but, more importantly, it would be dangerous to do so. Marchant would have replaced the officers, but if Bartlett hands had stayed on they might recognize him.

He made his way down the corridor until he found a recruiting table for a Marchant ship that hadn't come from their takeover of Bartlett.

A smiling woman greeted him. She nodded to the bag slung over his shoulder.

"Between berths?" she asked. "Looking for another?"

"I am," Jon said, "if the bargain's right."

The woman raised an eyebrow, as though unused to anyone suggesting there was a bargain to be made instead of simply accepting Marchant's terms.

"Ordinary spacer," she said. "One and twelve the month. Two-year contract."

Jon nodded. "I'm rated Able," he said, "and struck for master's mate on my last ship."

The documents Eades had supplied would back that up.

"You look young for Able."

The woman looked at him oddly and Jon realized he wasn't behaving as a merchant spacer.

Play the part, he told himself. *Hide the hatred and play the part.*

He forced a grin and leaned down to rest his elbows on the table.

"I've skills and more skills," he said. "Perhaps if we're not to be shipmates I could show you some of my others over a pint?"

The woman looked him over and chuckled. "You're a bit young for me, lad, and haven't nearly the parts I prefer."

Jon straightened and gave her a sheepish look. "Sorry, then ... but about a berth?"

"Able's two and seven, if the bosun approves you. You strike for master's mate if there's an opening, for we've none now."

"Fair enough."

The woman tapped on her tablet for a moment.

"You've your ratings?" she asked. "And your name?"

Jon nodded. He swiped his finger across his own tablet to send her his forged papers and ratings. He'd have to get used to the new name Eades had provided, as well.

"Name's Dansby," he said. "Avrel Dansby."

PART TWO

TWO

Jon's mother, Elizabeth, was in the kitchen overseeing the final details of the holiday dinner. He could smell the roasting turkey and spices even from two rooms away and debated, for a moment, sneaking in to weasel a bit of the bird, or perhaps an early slice of one of the pies.

Instead he made his way towards his father's study, where Edward was meeting with Uncle Wyatt.

He raised the toy ship he held above his head as he moved — model, really, as it was the concept model for Bartlett Shipping's latest flagship, *Elizabeth*, now being built at Greater Sibward's orbital shipyard.

Named for Jon's mother, the massive, four-masted ship was one of the largest on the Fringe, rivaling even the Marchant Company's huge merchantmen, and faster, for all its size. Much faster, if what Jon had heard was true.

At the study door, he cradled the ship under his arm — careful with the rigging, since Uncle Wyatt had impressed upon him how delicate the strands of plastic representing the ship's lines were — and reached up to key the latch.

The study's wood flooring was cold under his bare feet after the *carpeted runner in the hallway, so Jon rose up on tiptoe and hurried to the thick rug around his father's desk.*

"Why the delays?" his father asked.

"You know why, Edward," Uncle Wyatt said. "No matter the excuses the shipyard gives up."

"Hmph."

Jon reached up and set his ship carefully on the desktop and went around to his father's side of the desk.

"'Hmph' you may," Wyatt said, "but we should have expected this."

"No company should have such power, nor wield it like this."

Jon stopped beside his father's chair and held his arms up, which had the expected result of his being grasped and lifted up to rest in the broad lap that always welcomed him. He rested his face against his father's chest and smelled the familiar, comforting scents of spices, woods, and other goods from far-flung planets, so different from the scent of thermoplastic that clung to his mother after her trips to the shipyards.

"The Elizabeth's *a threat to them, and they know it. Her design's faster than any they have and they don't like that we have the patents and rights to that design."*

Edward sighed. "I know. And it might go easier for us if we just sold them the design, as they've asked."

"I'll speak well of you at the wake." Wyatt snorted. "Elizabeth'd have you in the oven next to the bird if you sold off her design like that."

"No doubt, but with the work stoppages and the Marchants buying up every bit of material we need, it'll be a miracle does her design ever taste darkspace."

"But once it does ..."

"Aye," Edward said, "once it does —"

His father's lap disappeared and Jon fell —

"UP AND OUT, Dansby, you lazy bugger!"

Jon —

No, Avrel Dansby, now, he reminded himself, even as his body crashed to the deck with a heavy *thump* and a sharp pain in his left wrist.

"*Up!*" the quartermaster's mate, Bridgeford, yelled, casting a heavy boot into Avrel's thigh.

"Aye! I'm up," Avrel said, scrambling to his feet. He shook the pain out of his wrist, along with the that of the faded dream, and edged away from Bridgeford — not so far that the crowd of watching crewmen could call him shy, but far enough that he'd be able to dodge Bridgeford's next kick or cuff, should it come. As well to keep from going for the man's throat, for the sight of Bridgeford in his Marchant Company shipsuit filled him with a rage as great as the peace the dream had brought. He'd never know that peace again in truth — with his father dead, mother indentured on an unknown world, and Uncle Wyatt gone into self-imposed exile on colony world.

Bridgeford scowled. "See that you are when the pipes sound next time."

He stalked away and Avrel wondered if the man would ever know just how close he'd come to having his head bashed against the bulkhead.

Avrel turned his own scowl on his messmates, who'd let him sleep through the quartermaster's call for all hands to make sail. Again.

"My thanks, lads," Avrel muttered to them as he smoothed the bedding on his bunk and folded it flush with the bulkhead above Sween's.

That worthy, the leader of their mess, at least in the eyes of the other members, Detheridge and Grubbs, grinned widely.

"Och, an' y'loooked so peaceful, y'did," he said, eyes wide and innocent. "'Ad a smile on yer face like a wee bairn an' we were loathe t'disturb ye, we were."

Avrel shrugged acceptance. He'd been sleeping heavier than he should, likely using it as an escape, he'd admit, and he couldn't blame his messmates for growing tired of waking him.

Pipes sounded over *Minorca's* speakers again and Avrel hurriedly latched his bunk to the bulkhead. Bridgeford was bad enough, but if the lot of them weren't out on the hull soon, the quartermaster himself would become involved, and none of them wanted to draw Hobler's notice, much less his ire.

"'Urry along, then, keelman," Sween prodded, making Avrel wince at the nickname. It was because of that bloody Eades he'd been saddled with it and he'd like a word or two with the man.

He slid the storage on his bunk's underside open and pulled out his vacsuit, then followed his mates as they rushed forward from the berthing deck to the sail locker at the ship's bow, slipping inside just as Bridgeford was sliding it closed. Even before the sound of the latch fastening sounded, Avrel and his mates had the seals on their vacsuits open.

The others in the sail locker already had their vacsuits on and watched the latecomers with open amusement.

Avrel sealed his own vacsuit to the neck. They'd all filled their air tanks when last they came in from outside, but he still checked the gauges on the back of each of his messmates' suits, as each of them checked his. The Dark was harsh and offered no mercy for the ill-prepared.

"Yer set," Sween muttered, as Avrel clapped a hand on Detheridge's shoulder to confirm her gages and hoses were correct as well.

The helmet was next, and Avrel could hear the quartermaster's voice was already sounding over his vacsuit radio as he made those seals tight, just before Bridgeford triggered the pumps to put the sail locker in vacuum.

"— last tack a'fore we transition, if we're lucky." Hobler chuckled, something he was more likely than not to do every time he spoke, no matter if he were calling for another round in some pub or yelling for some bloody lubber for moving up the mast with less alacrity than he felt appropriate. "Then it's a hop to Penduli Station and a bit of rest, lads, so make it a lively evolution, will you?"

Bridgeford shuffled through the crowd of spacers to the forward hatch, and the chorus of *Ayes* was cut off in a burst of static as he triggered the outer hatch. *Darkspace* radiation filled the now open locker, interfering with the electronics and killing their vacsuit radios.

Avrel filed out of the locker with the others, feeling the familiar hitch in his stomach as he stepped from the artificial gravity of the locker onto *Minorca's* hull.

He spared a glance further forward, past the ship's bowsprit, to the vast expanse of *darkspace* ahead of them. A black canvas, relieved only by the distant swirling of *darkspace* storms where the winds of dark energy picked up and made visible the dark matter that permeated everything here, like black foam picked from an ocean's wavetops.

There was little time for gawking at the view, though, as the crew rushed up the masts. Avrel clipped his own safety line to the mainmast and sprang upward with the others, floating alongside the thick pole of thermoplastic to the topsail booms, then pulling himself along that to his position.

Minorca was taking in sail, so as to slow her speed and be more maneuverable as she neared Penduli.

The azure glow of the charged sails sparked white as he grasped the thin metal mesh of the sails and pulled along with the other. They took in two reefs, hauling the metal in and wrapping it to the yard, then making it fast.

All in silence, responding only to each other's hand signals and those of the master's mates below on the hull. It was hot, heavy work and his vacsuit stank of the sweat of hours and days doing the same. Avrel took a pause in the work to look out at *darkspace* again and wonder what his life would have been like if it'd continued on its course instead of being derailed by the Marchants.

He jumped as something touched him and found Detheridge had scooted over on the yard far enough to touch her helmet to his.

"Stop lallygagging, lad," she said, "they're callin' us in."

Avrel glanced down to the hull and saw the rest of the crew was headed down the masts and making their way to the sail locker.

"We'll transition to normal-space soon," Detheridge went on. "Then it's leave on Penduli, so don't dally!"

ONCE *MINORCA* WAS MADE FAST to the station's quayside and the docking and cargo tubes made fast, Captain Morell called for all hands to assemble on the berthing deck.

Avrel shuffled into the crowd with the rest of the crew, near his messmates. Captain Morell and *Minorca's* two mates, Carr and Turkington, were on a slightly raised platform at the aft end of the deck, just forward of the wardroom and the captain's quarters aft of that.

Morell stepped to the edge of the platform and began speaking as soon as the quartermaster indicted that everyone was in attendance.

"Well, lads, I told you there'd be some changes once we made port at Penduli and we're here," Morell said, "so here's what we're doing.

"First, Mister Carr's off the ship for leave and we'll be getting a new second mate."

There were some uneasy looks and mutters at that, for the second mate dealt most directly with the crew, through the quartermaster. Carr was a good man and well-liked. He brooked no excuses, as was the norm for the Marchant Company as a whole, but he never worked the crew beyond reason.

Morell, as well, did not look pleased with the news he delivered, but went on.

"His replacement is enroute, but we're early, so you'll have a few more days leave here than expected." He hurried on as the crew perked up at that news. "And you'll need it," he said, instantly quelling the crew's excitement. "We've no more short hauls and easy routes ahead of us. Once Carr's replacement is aboard, we'll be setting sail to *Hso-Hsi* for a load of silks."

There was a moment's silence, then a cheer. Avrel looked around and most of the crew seemed to be expressing pleasure, if mixed with a bit of worry.

Hso-Hsi was a long haul for any ship, but *Minorca* was smaller than those that normally made that journey. They'd be feeling cramped by the time they finished, no doubt, and it would be a long finish coming — more than six months, at least, even though *Minorca* was a fast ship. The cargo, though, artificed-silk, was valuable enough that the crew's shares would be large.

The *Hissies* had managed to perfect a closely-held method of getting their silkworms to ingest virtually anything and combine it with the silk. From practical to luxury applications, the silks were much in demand. There was even a rumor that they'd managed to get the worms to eat gallenium, but, if true, the *Hissies* were holding that product even more closely — such a product would make everything from vacsuits to the netting over a ship's gunports more effective, and the value would be immense.

THE PENDULI STATION merchant quayside was a scene of self-organizing chaos.

Spacers filed on and off the ships nestled up to the station and connected with docking tubes. Carters moved containers of freight and supplies to and from the warehouses of the station's inner side, yelling and gesturing as some other got in their path. Vendors hawked their wares to those just coming off ships after weeks or months in the Dark — and amongst those were the younger hawkers, looking for someone to guide to the station's more dubious establishments.

Boys and girls rushed toward *Minorca's* debarking crew. They called out the offerings of the places which would give them the best commissions for leading a spacer there, expertly reading the faces of the spacers for interest, then zeroing in on them.

"Girls!" a boy called, rushing up to Sween and tugging at his hand.

Another grasped Detheridge's arm. "Come, lady! I'll show you the best place — you'll be happy. Broad shoulders, skin like bronze!"

One of them stared at Avrel for a moment, then stepped forward, knocking another boy aside. "Ignore these others, sir," he said. "Their houses have skinny girls, nothing but bones — put your eye out, they will." He stopped in front of Avrel and drew a shape in the air. "You need girl like pear — much nicer. Sweet and juicy."

"That's our Keelman," Sween called. "Every port they seem to know what he's after!"

Detheridge laughed. "I heard what you like, Dansby?" she asked. "A girl with a bit of a keel to her?"

Avrel flushed.

Detheridge laughed again. "Broad shoulders, you say?" she asked the boy who'd approached her.

"Like an ox, miss," he assured her.

"Well, then," she said, with a wink to Avrel. "I'll take that above the waist and you below, Dansby. Do have fun." She followed her new guide off into the crowd.

Avrel flushed darker, for he knew his messmates would likely give him guff about this. It wasn't his preference — and he'd prefer to keep those to himself, regardless — but there was only one person to blame.

He glared at the boy, who met his gaze confidently and with a cocky grin. Did he know the full of who he worked for? Likely not, only that he should approach a certain man from a certain ship and make a certain offer.

"All right, then," he said, making sure all of the other *Minorcas* had moved on and weren't close enough to overhear. "Take me to the bloody Pear."

The boy led off and Avrel followed. They quickly left the quay

Minorca had docked at and made their way around the station's ring. The look of what they passed through changed from the clean, ordered chaos of the Marchant docks, where the whole section of quay was leased to the company and available to no other ships, to something seedier and more disreputable.

Everything from the dress of the crews and dockworkers to the grime on the decks and bulkheads became noticeably worse the farther they went, and Avrel began noting the hard looks and narrowed eyes as he passed.

Marchant was not a well-liked company in some circles, and he'd have changed from his ship's jumpsuit with the distinctive logo if he'd known where the boy was leading him.

"Has your Pear no sense at all?" he hissed at the boy, but his question was met only with a shrug of indifference.

Of course, the boy turned inward midway through the worst of the quays Avrel had ever seen. Penduli was a large enough station that some parts fell naturally into disrepair. This was one such, near enough the Naval sector that it received some custom from the Navy's spacers who were looking for entertainments outside what was offered in their enclave. Those visits brought with them the Navy's Shore Patrol, and where the Patrol went, the Impressment Service was not far behind.

Merchants like the Marchant Company paid well to keep such things from the areas where their ships docked. For those merchantmen who couldn't, well, there was the reason for the quay's condition and low docking fees as well, wasn't there?

Avrel eyed the corridor the boy was leading him down dubiously. What lights there were flickered here and there, and access panels hung open where they'd been sprung and left hanging. Gaps were visible within those, where some of the station's own components had been taken, either for sale or for use on some long-left ship.

There was little signage about what sorts of establishments might be down that way, and what there was had been defaced with graffiti so often that the original words were all but unreadable — not that he'd trust the word of any signage in such a sector. The businesses here would be rather more mobile than signage could account for, and stubs of cut cables told the story of any digital signage that might have once been in place.

Avrel caught the odor as he drew near, and thought this section's facilities must be in as poor repair as the signage, if the smells were any indication.

"Come on, then," the boy called. "This way."

Avrel took a deep breath to steel himself, immediately regretted that, and considered tearing his ship's insignia off entirely.

Or telling the bloody Pear to take himself off to hell and be buggered by some demon.

THE ESTABLISHMENT they finally arrived at was much as Avrel expected it to be. Not, at least, the brothel he'd halfway feared, but a small, crowded pub of dubious origin.

Sandwiched between two other compartments, neither of which advertised what was inside and both with a hulking, narrow-eyed figure beside their hatches, was a narrow space. It appeared that those businesses to either side had commandeered some of the space, with haphazardly welded pieces of bulkhead making up the adjoining walls.

The space was even dimmer than the corridor and smelled worse — something Avrel wouldn't have credited if he'd not smelled it himself. A bit of the corridor mixed with rancid grease and whatever the pub had on offer for eating — all of which put Avrel far off of that.

The boy moved through the crowd easily, but Avrel was larger and there always seemed to be an elbow or shoulder he couldn't quite get around. Despite his care and muttered apologies, the shove and snarl of rage, when it came, was not unexpected.

"M'pint, y' lubberly bastard!" a man yelled, spinning to confront him after Avrel brushed against his elbow.

Avrel sighed and looked the man over. The pub's other patrons edged away, suddenly finding enough space to open a small circle around the pair. Long experience with such events made the crowd's movement appear choreographed.

He sighed again after getting a good look at his antagonist. Half a head shorter than Avrel, but with shoulders appearing as wide as he was tall, the man was clearly spoiling for a fight.

Detheridge might like those shoulders, if not for the face.

The fight the man was spoiling for was certainly not his first, for his nose had the mashed look of one which had been broken countless times. One eye was hooded and the eyebrow slashed through with scars. The knuckles around the pint glass were also visibly scarred, even in the poor light — and the glass itself was nearly full, meaning there'd been little spilled, if any, by Avrel's jostling. No, this was only an excuse to pummel a stranger.

Avrel wasn't a stranger to this sort of thing, at least not since leaving Lesser Sibward. First there'd been finding his place aboard ships with the crews — there was always a bit of jostling involved in that, and one had to fight for one's place. Or, at least, show a willingness to fight and not back down or be bullied. And if a fight was ordained, he'd quickly found, it was best finished quickly — no dancing about and certainly no fairness.

"I'll be happy to buy you a new pint —" Avrel ventured.

"Ha! 'Appy to buy me a pint,' he says." The man drained his glass at one go and narrowed his eyes. He flexed his shoulders in that way some men do to show they're preparing for some effort. "If yer happy t'buy a pint, lad, I'll make y' bloody ecstatic."

He handed his glass to someone in the crowd, never taking his eyes from Avrel, and stepped toward him.

Avrel moved as the man was midstep, snatching a full glass from the crowd and stepping forward himself. He swung the glass at the man's head while simultaneously driving his knee upward.

His target, concentrating on the glass and its contents being swung at his head, missed the knee and let out a pained grunt as it connected with his fork. He did manage to block Avrel's swing, but not the flung glass, which broke against the side of his head.

The blow to his bollocks doubled him over and Avrel, as though running in place, was already bringing his other knee up to connect with the man's face — helped along with a hand to the back of the head.

There was a squishy crunch as the oft-broke nose met its fate once more, and Avrel finished the move by driving his elbow into the side of the man's head where the glass had struck.

He danced backward, leaving his opponent to collapse to the floor.

"Stay down," Avrel said, as the man got his hands under him.

"You little bug —"

Avrel didn't wait for him to finish. He stepped forward, swinging his heavy, metal-toed boot into the man's ear, crushing and tearing cartilage and skin.

This time the man stayed down, but Avrel didn't relax. Instead he stayed light on his feet, knowing that now would be the time for any friends the man had to come to his aid.

He relaxed a bit as the crowd, which had edged farther away from the fight, began murmuring and broke up to return to their tables and the bar. One stayed behind, though — the one the fallen man had handed his glass to.

This man eyed Avrel for a moment, then snorted. He set the empty glass next to the unconscious man's head.

"Should'a took the pint, mate."

Avrel relaxed a bit and looked for the boy, who was still farther back in the pub looking on with amusement.

"You coming, then?" the boy asked.

Avrel scanned the crowd and relaxed more. Whatever dislike they might have for a Marchant crewman, if not dissolved, had then been overlaid with caution.

He did wonder at the place, though. His meetings with Eades' proxies — a half-dozen of them in as many systems since he'd signed aboard with Marchant — had all been in far nicer places than this one. It made him wonder what sort of low-life scum Eades had working for him on Penduli, that he chose such a place.

It was all the more perplexing, then, as he followed the boy to the rear of the pub, down an access corridor, dank from a leaking water pipe, into one of the pub's storerooms — only to find the man himself.

***

"AH, MISTER BARTLETT," Eades said, smiling widely. "How good of you to come."

The storage room was crowded with containers of pub supplies, stacked deck to deck in some cases, and a small desk to one side, almost as an afterthought.

Eades, smiling and unremarkable as ever, sat at the desk and gestured for Avrel to sit, though Eades had the only chair. Opposite the desk was only a pair of containers, too high for a proper chair and making an awkward seat.

Avrel narrowed his eyes. He'd not met with Eades, nor heard from him directly, since signing aboard with the Marchants on Greater Sibward. Always before it had been the man's agents, taking his reports on whichever system Avrel's ship arrived at — seemingly always aware of his coming, and greeting his arrival with that bloody code Eades found so very clever.

"About your bloody code phrase," Avrel began, determined to address that first, so long as the man himself was here. He'd had enough of the looks.

"That will be all, Samarth," Eades said. "Mister Bartlett will be quite able to find his way back on his own."

The boy, Samarth, nodded and left, sliding the hatch shut behind him.

Eades raised his brow. "'Code phrase'?"

"Yes, this bloody 'pear' business. Every port I come to, there's some boy leading me away while he extols the virtues of some imaginary girl's bottom." He scowled. "I'll thank you to choose something else, now I have you here."

"But, Mister Bartlett, it's so clever, given your name, is it not?"

"It's bloody silly!"

Eades' brow raised further. "And what quality or service would you rather my lads offer you? Something you'd rather your mates think your interest lies? Oh, I have it, we'll use —"

"No!" Avrel cut him off hurriedly, suddenly horrified at the possibilities. "Now I think of it, 'pear' will do nicely. No need to change it. Not a bit."

Eades smiled. "I thought as much." He sat back in his chair and motioned for Avrel to sit again. "We may begin, then — tell me what *Minorca's* been up to, Mister Bartlett."

Avrel sighed. It did seem that Eades always got his way, usually by arranging things so that his target had no real choice in the matter. He perched himself on the stacked crates, finding them just ever so slightly off balance, so that, while they were a natural and not unreasonable place to sit, part of his attention would forever be on not toppling over.

Likely planned this way, as well.

He stood again, took the top crate off and set it aside, then sat on the one remaining. He was low to the ground and looking up at Eades like a child sent to the schoolmaster, but at least he could have his full wits about him.

Eades smiled again, as though pleased, and that made Avrel wonder that even in the unstacking he'd been manipulated again somehow.

Damn the man, but he makes one feel as a rat in his bloody maze.

"The seating is to your liking now, Mister Bartlett?"

Avrel cleared his throat. "Just get on with it, will you? And hadn't you best not use my real name?"

"There's no one here to hear, and Samarth is utterly loyal to me." Eades' smile fell. "As well, I wish to remind you, perhaps, of who you really are and what you're about this."

"Do you think I don't?" Avrel felt his face flush with anger.

There was not a day, not an hour, aboard *Minorca* that he didn't feel his hatred for the Marchant Company and what they'd done. It was all he could do sometimes to contain the urge to overload the ship's fusion plant and send the bloody lot to hell. Only the knowledge that neither the crew nor even the officers were to blame for what the Company had done to his family kept him from it — that and the certainty that a single ship would be no loss to the Marchants.

No, he longed to hurt them, but far more than the loss of a single ship.

"There's the spark," Eades whispered. "There's the glint in your eye." He stood suddenly and pried open the lid of a nearby container. "Oh, what luck —"

He pulled out a bottle, looked around the storeroom for a moment, then removed a second, setting both on the desk, one before Avrel and one before himself.

He sat again, removed the bottle's cap, and, with an absurd amount of delicacy for drinking from a bottle's neck, took a sip.

"Do help yourself — I assure you the proprietor is well compensated. I see no glasses, but wouldn't necessarily trust them here and, well, when in Rome, yes?" He took another drink and pursed his lips. "It's quite fine — Irish, I'm afraid, but one can't have everything."

Avrel sighed and took up the bottle. He could almost wish it were one of Eades' agents and not the man himself, now, as the agents, at least, had a more practical manner. They didn't rush off on any tangent that might make them feel themselves clever. He took up the bottle, seeing that it was, indeed, a fine brand of whiskey, if Irish, as Eades said, and raised it to his lips.

"*Minorca's* actions?" Eades prompted, just as the whiskey entered Avrel's mouth. "That is why we're here, after all."

Avrel forced himself not to react. Jumping from tangent to the point and making the other fellow feel guilty for being on the path he'd just been led down was another of the man's infuriating tactics.

He held the drink in his mouth for a moment before swallowing, just to be certain Eades would know he wasn't rushing.

"You have the reports from your agent on Bidfield, yes? Well, then, since leaving there ..."

THE RECITATION of the Marchant ship's sails and trading since his last report took only a short time. There was little, in fact, of any import.

Minorca was a relatively small ship for the Marchants, and dedicated to shorter routes within New London space. She was not one of the truly massive ships the company used to ply *darkspace* to *Hso-hsi* and farther — which was why Avrel saved the news of their next destination for the last, filling Eades' ear with the trivial details of a hold full of produce and raw materials before announcing his news.

"And now we've sold all that off here on Penduli and the captain's announced our next destination —" He trailed off, anticipating Eades' reaction when he went on.

"*Hso-hsi*, yes," Eades said blandly, "but that's of no import."

Avrel blinked.

"You knew?"

Eades smiled. "I know most of what you report, dear boy. More than you report in nearly all cases, including this one. No, *Minorca's* destination is not the crucial bit, though you might have thought so — the crucial bit is your ship's *journey*."

Avrel raised an eyebrow at that, but stayed silent. He'd learned well enough that Eades needed to let on how very clever he was. The man would eventually get to his point, if left alone.

"From Penduli to *Hso-hsi*, your ship will be sailing through the Barbary. You'll take on some unimportant cargo of manufactured goods here at Penduli — something those benighted worlds of the Barbary will find useful, I'm sure — but those will be disposed of early on." His eyes narrowed. "What I want word of — and what you must get word of to me as quickly as it occurs, no matter the risk — is what cargo *Minorca* takes aboard next."

"Next?"

"Well, perhaps not immediately, but there will be a cargo in the Barbary of interest to me. And when it's taken aboard, you must inform one of my agents as quickly as possible." Eades paused. "Even at risk of exposing yourself."

"Now see here —"

"Mister Bartlett, do you wish to damage the Marchants? Hurt them as they've hurt you?"

"I do, but how does one cargo matter? Smuggling, even the worst of it, will be fobbed off on the captain, not the company. If I'm exposed, I'll be put off the ship and my image and records put about — no amount of your magic name-changing will ever get me aboard another Marchant ship."

Avrel glared at Eades. He'd thought the man more dedicated to harming the Marchants than this, which was why he'd helped him. Now it appeared Eades was nothing more than some petty police-man, on about a bit of smuggled goods. One cargo, even the worst Avrel could think of, would have no real impact on the Marchants. They'd simply blame Captain Morell and dismiss him.

"One cargo may be blamed on a captain, yes," Eades said, "but there have been others. Each one is a pebble — the bits of a mountain-side that tremble and clickety-clack down the slope in prelude to it all tumbling. I have a great many pebbles already and you, Mister Bartlett, with word of this cargo, will bring me the first great stone to set in motion."

"What cargo, then? What am I looking for?"

"You will know it when it comes, Mister Bartlett. You will have no doubt."

MINORCA REMAINED idle for two more days, Captain Morell

growing more and more visibly agitated all the while. After that time, the expected Marchant packet came, and along with it their new second mate.

Hobler once more assembled the crew on the berthing deck and Morell assembled his officers on the raised platform to one end.

Avrel jostled along with the rest, alternately trading barbs with Detheridge over which of them would miss a partner's broadness more when the ship finally left Penduli.

"I'm sure you'll —" Avrel cut off as he caught sight of the platform and its occupants.

One of them was both new to *Minorca* and one Avrel knew well. She'd cut her hair, it was far shorter now, and she held herself with more confidence than she had at school, but Avrel would never in life mistake the figure of Kaycie Overfield for anyone else.

"What's the matter, lad?" Detheridge asked. "You see a ghost?"

Avrel started a grin to put her off, realized his lips were trembling as much as his hands, and clenched his jaw instead.

He ducked his head and pressed hands to his stomach, both to hide his face from the assembled officers and put Detheridge off.

"A bit of the gripes," he muttered.

"Ah," Detheridge nodded. "Too much of Penduli's curries, I wager." She clapped a hand on Avrel's back. "A week on ship's commons'll set you right."

Avrel nodded, grateful that Morell had started speaking to introduce *Minorca's* new officer and Detheridge was distracted.

He wished he could say the same about Kaycie, as she was scanning the assembled crew, a polite smile on her face.

It was her, he was certain. But how was she here? Her family had their own ships and she was set to learn that business and take over after schooling, just as Avrel had been. Had been, before the Marchants took it all away — which certainly couldn't have happened to Kaycie. Not and have her here, working for the Marchants and being introduced with her real name as Morell did now.

How is she here?

Avrel's guts clenched in real pain. Kaycie was the one person beside his family who'd haunted Avrel's thoughts since he'd taken his new name. Wynne had been a good schoolmate, but that was all — the sort one might have a drink with once a decade and reminisce — but Kaycie ...

Well, he'd always wanted more of her, and thought there might be, at the end, when he'd gone aboard the school's boat to flee. There'd been no chance to contact her, though, and he'd had nothing to offer her if he could. Nothing to offer, and the fear that she might, if she knew of his circumstances, offer him some place in her own family's company. A thing he couldn't accept — both because it would be a charity he couldn't stomach and as it would keep him from pursuing his revenge against the Marchants.

Now she was here, though, and his plans were all upended.

How is she here, and how do I keep her from recognizing me?

Even as he thought that, it became useless. Kaycie was speaking, thanking the crew for their welcome — a bit of applause Avrel only dimly noted — and saying how pleased she was to be aboard one of the Marchant's finest ships. Her eyes scanned the crew, Avrel ducked his head, but kept his eyes on her — it had been so long since he'd seen her and she did look so fine in her uniform, as he'd always known she would.

Her eyes locked with his, lowered head and all, and he couldn't hide from her, no matter the cost. He raised his head and she stopped speaking, frowning.

Be clever, my girl, as clever as I know you to be, he prayed.

Kaycie resumed speaking, kept scanning the crowd, but her eyes returned to Avrel's time and time again.

"Thank you all again," she said, her eyes locked with Avrel's now as she finished. "As second mate has charge of the crew, I'll be meeting with each of you privately to learn the ways of the ship."

Morell's and Turkington's brows raised at that, as well as no few of the crew. That wasn't the norm, but a new officer would have her ways — only Avrel suspected the real reason, and blessed her for it, knowing that she must suspect he had some reason for being aboard this ship and not under his own name.

———————————

IT WAS A WEEK, though, before Kaycie's promised meetings took place. A week of hard sailing where officers and crew alike were too exhausted — and too likely to be called back to the sails — for any hope of meetings.

Minorca sailed the day after Kaycie's arrival, but once in *darkspace* found the system winds were strong, blowing heavily toward the system's primary.It was day after day of tacking against them before the ship was out of the system, away from those effects, and into the more variable winds between systems. Only then did the calls of *all hands to the sails* cease and the crew was able to get a proper rest when they were off watch.

True to her word, Kaycie called each of the crew to her cabin, and — if puzzled by the new experience of a tot of rum and a bit of a chat in a Marchant officer's cabin — they seemed to take to it.

Of Avrel's mess, Detheridge was the first to be called.

"She's a right one, if I'm any judge," she said upon her return and Grubbs' call. "Pours a full measure, in any case, and not of any swill, neither."

Avrel squared his shoulders and took a deep breath. He suspected he'd be next, and in no more than a quarter hour, as that seemed to be the time Kaycie was spending with each member of the crew. Unless she called on Sween next, in which case he'd have a full bell to sweat on it and wonder what she'd say. Would she turn him in to Captain Morell? He didn't think so, not after he explained himself — but there was still her working for the Marchants in the first place, which he couldn't fathom. Might she have changed so much in the years since school? He didn't think so, wouldn't credit it — not Kaycie. She was a solid mate, she'd not —

"What's in you, Dansby?" Detheridge asked. "You're squirming like a lad at his first brothel."

"I —"

Grubbs came out of the companionway hatch, with the slight list and owl-like expression he always had as he adjusted the first bit of drink in his hold.

"Dansby! She'll have you next."

Avrel swallowed and stared at the hatch as though it was the gate to hell itself.

"I'll go again if you've no mind to," Detheridge said. "I'd not say no to a second wet."

He took a deep breath and walked through the gate.

THE SECOND MATE'S cabin was small, by any measure but the space each of the crew had aboard *Minorca*. Compared to the tiered bunks and drawers of the crew's berth, the two-meter square compartment was palatial.

As the hatch slid shut behind him, Kaycie rose from the thin-backed stool she'd been seated on at the fold-down corner desk. Her bunk was folded up against the bulkhead for more space and a second stool sat in the corner opposite her desk.

Avrel had no more time to take in the surroundings, though, for after a single moment of staring at him, Kaycie flung herself across the small space.

Her arms wrapped around him and her face buried itself in his chest.

"It is you," she whispered again and again, her breath hot through his ship's jumpsuit.

"Kaycie, I —"

She cut him off by squeezing him harder, almost leaving him unable to breathe. His own arms went around her.

She pushed herself away from him. Away and then she backed to the far bulkhead, close as it was in the tiny compartment. She put her back to it and crossed her arms, as though trying to get as far from him as she'd just been pulling him close.

"*I thought you were dead!*"

Avrel winced and flushed hot. There was so much pain in her voice. Pain and accusation.

"There was no word," she whispered. "Not for so long. Both Wynne and I thought ..." Her face twisted with pain and anger. "We thought we'd helped you to your death in the Dark!" She swiped at her eyes. "And then the boat was back on the school's quay and nothing said about it, so we knew you'd made it somewhere. *And still there was no word!*"

Avrel's gaze fell to the deck. There was so much hurt in her voice. He hadn't thought of what his friends would think, what they'd wonder at when there was no word from him. He'd been so focused on finding a way to hurt the Marchants — and then, once aboard a Marchant ship, there'd been no safe way to tell them.

"There was —"

"*Don't you dare!* Don't you dare say there was no way to get us a word — not one single word? Not when you arrived at Greater Sibward? Nor while you were there? Nor once in the last *three years?*"

Kaycie grasped the back of her stool, spun it toward her, and fell heavily onto it, head bowed as though all the strength had been taken from her.

"I thought you were dead."

Avrel resisted the urge to go to her and lay an arm over her shoulders. He felt she'd not welcome that. He sat in the other stool, shoulders slumped, as weary as Kaycie looked.

"I'm sorry. I didn't think —"

Kaycie's head shook.

"Of course not, you were being Jon Bartlett." She sighed. "You had some plan, I imagine. Some bit of business, and thought nothing of anything but that." She wiped her eyes, still looking down, then only raised her gaze when they'd been thoroughly scrubbed of tears and the only evidence Avrel could see was their red rims. "So, what was it, then?"

"What?"

"Your plan. What you've been about. Tell me."

And just as though the last three years hadn't happened, though Avrel suspected he'd not heard the last of it from her on that, he was with Kaycie again. No Wynne, of course, but it was so much like being back at Lesser Sibward and planning some bit of fun again that his heart lightened — perhaps for the first time since that awful moment in the headmaster's office when he'd learned of his family's ruin.

He told Kaycie all that had happened. From leaving school, to finding there was nothing for him on Greater Sibward, to signing aboard ship. He left out the bits about Eades in the telling, and his plans for the Marchants, as well. Those were things Kaycie oughtn't know about. No matter how much being with her again might feel like school, this wasn't some prank he was about and he'd not drag her into it.

"Why?" she asked when he seemed to be finished.

Avrel shrugged.

Kaycie frowned.

"No, I can see you feeling you had no place and signing aboard ship. I can even understand your wishing a new name, though how you managed it I note you put a shine on ... but why a Marchant ship? For god's sake, Jon, of all the shipping companies about, why would you sign with Marchant if you thought they were behind ..." She closed her eyes and sighed heavily. "Of course. What else would Jon Bartlett do but play the fool after vengeance?" Her eyes narrowed. "What are you about, Jon? This isn't school anymore, this is a real ship a'sail in the Dark. Your pranks could have real consequences out here, and hurt real people."

Avrel flushed. She was speaking to the Jon Bartlett she remembered as a schoolboy, not the Avrel Dansby who'd been three years aboard Marchant ships doing a man's work and making his plans. She'd grown, herself, in those three years to become an officer aboard ship, but gave him no credit for the time.

"I'm not about any pranks," he said.

"I imagine not, but you've vengeance in mind, I have no doubt either — and whatever sabotage you have in mind could harm the ship or crew. What is it?"

"Am I speaking to my friend or *Minorca's* second mate?"

Kaycie looked pained. "Your ... friend, Jon. Always that." She swallowed. "I'd not see you hurt, nor regret hurting others."

Avrel nodded. There might be something else in her voice, something he couldn't place, but he believed her. Whatever might have brought her to the Marchants instead of her own family's ships, she was still his friend.

"I'm planning no sabotage," he told her. "Not of the ship, at least."

And so, he told her of Eades and their arrangement. Of passing along what information he had to Eades' agents when approached, and what Eades had done to get him his new identity.

Kaycie's brow furrowed while he spoke and she frowned heavily.

"Foreign Office? Are you certain of that?"

Avrel shrugged. "As I may be. The identity he supplied is solid and his network of agents make me think he must be. He's his fingers into nearly everything, in any case, and knows too much not to have some government support behind him." He shrugged again. "For the moment, our interests are aligned, regardless of who he may be." He paused. "You'll have to call me by my new name, you know?"

Kaycie nodded. "Where the crew might hear, I will. In private you'll always be my Jon, and I'll not change that."

Avrel smiled. He still wished that might be true in fact, but doubted she meant it the way he might.

Kaycie was silent for a time and Avrel took the opportunity to ask his own question.

"And you? What's happened with you since school? What brought you aboard a Marchant ship instead of your family's?"

Kaycie chuckled but there was no mirth in it.

"I spent the year after school aboard family ships. It was a quite happy time." Her face hardened. "But the Overfields have no ships any longer, Jon, we were bought out last year."

"Bought out?"

"It was a fair offer, though not one the family would have accepted in other circumstances."

A chill went through Avrel at her words.

"They did manage to arrange for our ships' officers to be taken on by the new owners. All were transferred to other ships almost immediately, of course, so that there'd not be Overfields commanding former Overfield ships — that wouldn't do, I suppose."

She met Avrel's eyes and he saw the same hard look she'd had when she drove her foot into York Scoggins' fork.

"And so, you'll understand, Jon, when I say that I should like to meet your Mister Eades at the gentleman's very earliest convenience."

MINORCA MOVED on from Penduli into the Barbary.

For Avrel and the other spacers, without access to the quarterdeck and the navigation console there, little changed. Their work outside the hull in the featureless expanse of *darkspace* went on as usual.

Their arrival at Kuriyya was much like any port, though certainly more like one of the Fringe's younger colonies than any Core world, as there was no station circling above Kuriyya for them to make fast to. All of the goods from Penduli must be brought down to the surface in *Minorca's* boats and unloaded in-atmosphere at the planet's main town. On a landing field with half its surface still dirt and grass, no less, and that far better for their boats and work than the jaggedly cracked expanse of paving left on the field.

"Bloody barbarians can't pave a bloody field," Detheridge muttered, as they stumbled their way across the rutted field. *Minorca's* anti-grav cart might keep itself level over the terrain, but their boots had no such advantage. "And why's it all the bloody cargo on this bloody world?" She grunted and heaved a shoulder against the cart to slide it away from a low berm the sensors had decided was too steep to navigate.

Avrel shared a look with Sween and both hid a grin. With Detheridge's mood and punctuating her words with 'bloody' so much, she'd be taking out her frustrations when *Minorca's* crew was done and had an evening's leave. She'd leave someone bloody, sure enough, whether she spent her time in a pub or brothel, they knew.

Her question had merit, though, and Avrel was pondering that very thing. He'd been brought up to measure a cargo's worth, and the goods *Minorca'd* carried from Penduli would certainly have more value deeper into the Barbary. To sell it all at their first stop and rely on locally produced goods for the rest of their trip to *Hso-hsi* made little sense to him. Better to spread it out, or travel far deeper before selling — Kuriyya was just on the periphery, after all.

Detheridge stopped, stretched to ease her back, and wiped her brow.

"Bloody planets," she muttered. "Never the same bloody temperature twice in a row, how they stand it I'll never bloody fathom."

FOR A BLESSING AND A CURSE, there was no boy pulling Avrel's hand and prattling about pears as *Minorca's* crew exited the boat for their leave. He caught Kaycie's eye and shook his head slightly, letting her know that there was no chance of her meeting Eades on Kuriyya — and now likely no chance until their return to New London space. The man himself wouldn't travel deep into the

Barbary or to *Hso-hsi*, and his agents would have neither cause nor authority to trust Kaycie.

So, they went their separate ways for the evening's leave. That was a disappointment. Other than the one private meeting in Kaycie's cabin, there were no opportunities for them to speak privately aboard *Minorca*. Such contact between an officer and crewman would be remarked on, and no matter how private they thought themselves, the cramped quarters aboard ship would always provide that someone would overhear or see.

Neither could they be seen together on leave. On a larger world or station they might make arrangements to meet far from the landing field or quay, but Kuriyya's port town was so small that there was too much risk of being seen.

Instead they wandered separately, Avrel following along behind a group of *Minorca's* crew, but not really part of them. His own mess-mates had split up as well, Detheridge having other interests than Sween and Grubbs.

The town's streets were dimly and variably lit, the streetlights' solar panels being old and ill-kept.

The sewers were equally ill-kept, it seemed, for the street — such as it was, having its deteriorated paving mostly torn up to expose bare earth — ran with refuse and worse.

Someone had invested more than a little in Kuriyya once, for it to have such things at all, but whatever the source of those funds had been, they'd clearly disappeared long ago. Odd they didn't keep things up, though, as there were enough ships in-system even now that a bit of a landing fee would pay for the upkeep well enough.

All of the pubs and other establishments had ample customers, and the streets, though not crowded, were certainly not empty themselves.

The last of the group Avrel followed turned into a pub, but Avrel kept on.

An odd melancholia fell over him — or perhaps it had been there for some time and he only now became aware of it.

His thoughts turned to what his life might have been, if the Marchants had not destroyed his future. Perhaps he'd be walking on some world with Kaycie Overfield now. Not officer and crew aboard a Marchant ship, but officers of their own families' fleets — equals and having no fear of being seen together and caught out.

They might even, he fancied, come to some understanding. The spark of interest he'd noted when she saw him off from Lesser Sibward, and the degree of concern when she thought him dead, made him think there might be something to her feelings for him other than mere friendship. He knew his own feelings ran deeper.

One of the pubs had opened a window onto the street, selling out-sized mugs of their wares and Avrel stopped to buy one. It wasn't anything he'd seen before, but tasted of rum and what he suspected was some local fruit.

She was such a clever girl. Just look at how she'd caught sight of him for the first time aboard *Minorca* and not cried out as some might, then put together a plan on the spot for how to speak to him privately. He might have come up with the plans for pranks back at school, but she was always the best at refining them — teasing out the details so that there was less risk.

He wandered aimlessly, though instinctively keeping to the spacers' quarter and away from the darker alleys or less-travelled routes. Those on the streets around him grew more boisterous as the night went on — and as the air grew cooler, Avrel noted with some relief. Detheridge had been spot on in that complaint, and Avrel shared her inability to fathom how those in-atmosphere stood the variations.

He noted that many of the pubs had open windows selling wares, and that his mug was empty, so he stopped at the next. It was a different drink, but he turned over the few coins-cost without asking its contents. His mood had not improved with the first mug, but that was no reason to cease trying.

His thoughts returned to Kaycie, and his head filled with images of her even as his second mug emptied.

Her upturned nose. Her hair, cut short now, but flowing long back at Lesser Sibward — and both, if he were to be honest, quite fetching in their own way. The little furrow between her eyes which told one she was cross and not to be trifled with on some matter. The feel of her arms around him and her breath hot against his chest.

He drained his mug, noted it was not quite the same as what he remembered his second to have been, wondered at that a bit, but spied another window which yielded a refill of some sort.

What had he been thinking about again? Oh, yes, Kaycie. He'd had it bad for her at Lesser Sibward, he had to admit, but he'd reconciled that she didn't want him. Then there was that kiss as he'd left, which left him all in irons — but nothing for it, as he'd likely never see her again. Until now — and still, no chance for them. Not aboard ship, not with him in the crew and her a ship's officer.

The night had turned chill somehow and the streets were less full than earlier. He had no idea of the time, but *Minorca* wasn't due to leave until the following afternoon. The crew merely had to be aboard by the end of the forenoon watch and that would surely be no difficulty.

He sighed. This wandering was doing him no —

A man's voice drew Avrel's attention. He stood before a dark building with shrouded windows. Deep red light leaked around the windows' edges and the silhouettes applied to the glass made the establishment's purpose clear.

The man said something else incomprehensible, then squinted at Avrel.

"Londoner, yes?"

Avrel nodded, eyes on the establishment's door, struggling with a sudden urge.

"'Have a go,' yes? As you say, yes?"

A deep draught from his mug emptied most of it, then another to finish it off. He nodded and returned the man's smile.

"Aye."

Inside a woman met him, scantily dressed but past her prime for such a place and now set to greeting until a client with that particular fancy came about.

She took in Avrel's dress and read his ships' patch with a practiced eye.

"Welcoming," she said with a wide smile. "What it is you like, yes?"

Avrel wondered for a moment how many languages she and the man outside might speak. The Barbary was ostensibly part of Hanover, so many of the settlers would be German, but it also drew the flotsam from whatever ships passed through and whatever men must flee so far away. She'd likely learned enough of as many languages as she needed to serve those who came.

He broke off his musing as his eyes adjusted. The interior was darker than the street, even with it being night and the streetlights so dim. Now he could make out more than shadows and saw a half dozen girls, all clad to draw the attention they catered to.

They lounged about, each watching him and posing to catch his eye.

"You wish?" the woman asked, gesturing to the girls.

Avrel set his mug on the side-table near the door, it was empty now.

"Yes," he said, "someone ..." He swallowed. "Someone slight." *No bloody pears tonight.* "And ... hair to here." He brought his hand to his head to show her, flushing as he did so. This was ... not right, somehow, but some part of him pushed forward regardless. "Perhaps a nose that turns up, just a bit and a crease just —"

A girl coming down the stairs drew Avrel's eye. She was close — so close. Not exactly, but she'd do.

Make do. Minorca *to make do for my own ship, revenge to make do for a family, and this ... her ...* He nodded to the girl on the stairs and smiled as was expected of him. She'd know, of course, what he was doing. That was part of the arrangement, after all, and there was something of a higher service in that. She'd do her best to fill one of the holes that *Minorca*, vengeance, and she, never truly could.

The greeter smiled wider, seeing he'd made his choice. She gestured him toward the stairs even as the girl smiled wider as well and cocked her head coyly.

Make do.

MINORCA'S HOLD was echoingly empty despite the mass of men and bustle of activity. The scent of hot thermoplastic permeated the air, both from the carpenter's shop, aft, and the work being done forward, where Avrel was, with the rest of the crew, transforming the vast open space of the hold.

That scent was making Avrel's stomach churn — at least that was what he blamed it on, and not his drinking of the night before. The echoing shouts of the crew and their ongoing work was also making his head pound, and his arms ached from lifting the heavy bulkheads and holding them in place.

Nearly all the crew was working on the task, with the quartermaster and his mates, as well as Kaycie, overseeing the work.

They had large sheets of bulkhead printed by the carpenter and his machines, and were busy erecting them to form compartments all down the length of the hold. Each was a bit less than two meters' square, with a solid, locking hatch.

After the bulkheads were hefted into place, they were welded to the deck and overhead — then another crew entered with long, narrow planks of thermoplastic and welded them as some sort of shelving to the interior of the new compartment.

It was perplexing Avrel, because nearly all cargo came aboard already in its own chests and containers, usually sealed by the shipper — or Captain Morell himself if it was a cargo he'd bought for company profit. He'd never seen anything that needed its own compartments and shelving, especially such odd shelving, for these ran the full length of the compartment and from deck to overhead, with less than a third of a meter between them. The space in each compartment's center was barely enough for a man to enter and turn around in.

He sighed and lowered his arms as the last of the preliminary welds were completed on his current bulkhead. It would stay in place now, but it was time to move on to the next.

He closed his eyes for just a moment, jaw clamped tight against the nausea and willing his head to stop its pounding for a just a moment, if it pleased.

"Mister Hobler!" Kaycie called out.

Avrel hoped it might be a bit of a break, though it was early for that, but Kaycie had a kind heart and she'd know many of the crew were feeling poorly after their night's liberty on Kuriyya's surface. Avrel himself had found himself bundled up by Hobler's mates as they made the rounds of the port to collect any of the crew who'd overindulged the night before.

He remembered going upstairs with the girl and then there'd been more drink and ... well, what one did with such girls ... he supposed ... the whole of it was a bit blurry in his recollection, if he were honest.

The morning — afternoon, really — was clear. He'd been fast asleep, in one of a row of chairs in the house's kitchen, propped between two other spacers who'd not had the wherewithal to leave on their own when their business was done. Luckily it was Hext in charge of the party collecting him and not Bridgeford, for Hext had a bit of a heart. He'd not had any of his crew deliver an extra blow or two as they dumped Avrel onto their antigrav cart with two other moaning *Minorcas* and trundled the lot back to the landing field.

Other than that, the night before was a jumbled mess of images, half-remembered sounds, and more than a few sensations he really did wish he *could* remember better ...

He flushed at what memories he did have, though, for there was a fuzzy image of nuzzling into warm, soft skin while murmuring Kaycie's name. The girl'd been understanding, playing along as he was sure she'd done a thousand times with others, but it was still an embarrassing memory for him to —

"See to it that man understands the time for his daydreams was on leave and not while there's ship's work to be done!"

"Aye, miss!" Hobler called.

Avrel yelped as something struck his head with a dull *thud*.

He opened his eyes to find Bridgeford grinning at him, his starter — a short length of ship's line, knotted at one end — raised for another blow.

"Not to the *head*, Bridgeford!" Kaycie yelled. "That one's addled enough as it is!"

Avrel took in Bridgeford's glee, Hobler's stern glare, and, perplexing as to why, Kaycie's own narrowed eyes and thin lips. Bloody hell, but what'd he done to upset her so and have her set the quartermaster's mates on him?

He yelped again as Bridgeford's starter *thudded* into his backside.

"Aye, miss!" he called, and hurriedly moved on to where the next bulkhead waited to be put into place. "Working, miss!"

LUNCH with his messmates was a surly, growling affair.

Avrel's stomach alternated between rumbling demands for food and balking as each bite arrived, the clatter and muted voices from the other messes did nothing for his head, and his back and buttocks ached from more than one well-placed blow of Bridgeford's starter. He seethed a bit at that last, for Kaycie'd seemed to take a perverse glee in pointing him out every time he slacked or slowed in the work.

And truly he hadn't slacked *that* much after the first blows. He'd kept his wits about him, but she'd called him out for every bit of a breather he'd taken, and Bridgeford'd made it his mission to be well-placed for the calls.

What the bloody hell had he done to displease her so? It was not as though they'd so much as spoken since that first meeting in her cabin. Other than orders and niceties there was little reason for common crew such as himself to have words with a ship's officer, certainly not private ones, so their contact had been necessarily limited.

Yet all day she'd been glaring at him every time he glanced at her and setting him a beating at every opportunity.

He took another bite, chewing slowly in the hopes his stomach would take the warning that more was coming and prepare itself better than the last.

Opposite him and Grubbs at the narrow table they shared, which folded down from the bulkhead on which their narrow bunks were stacked four-high, Sween and Detheridge bumped elbows and Detheridge swore as a few drops of her grog ration spilled from her cup.

"Watch yourself!"

"You watch yer own bloody self!" Sween shot back.

Detheridge swapped her mug to her off hand and drove an elbow into Sween's side.

"I'll watch you buggered if you don't mind your space!" she said.

Sween turned toward her on his share of the bench and looked to draw his arm back for a real blow.

"What's into you two?" Avrel demanded. "Knock it off — I've had enough attention from Hobler's mates today, damn you!"

Detheridge and Sween turned their ire across the table.

"And aren't we painted with your idling brush, as well?" Detheridge asked. "You think Bridgeford'll not be watching all of us, now he knows you've gone and pissed in the little miss' grog?"

"And how'd you manage that, lad?" Sween asked. "She's been fair as can be since she come aboard, but now she's started a shit-list, sure. And it's your name all the bloody way down."

"I wish I knew," Avrel muttered.

"Well find out and fix it, boy," Detheridge said. "Things are bad enough without we're splattered with your leavings."

Avrel frowned.

"What's bad enough?" he asked. "And what's got into you two, as well, with your squabbling?" He turned to Grubbs, who'd spent the whole of the meal with downcast eyes, shoveling food into his mouth and speaking nary a word. "And you, you're silent as well." His whole mess was out of sorts and had been for the entire day. He, at least, had the excuse of far too much drink the night before, but the other three weren't known for excess in that. He'd never seen them come back from leave so out of sorts before. "What's the matter?"

"*What's the matter?*" Detheridge hissed.

Grubbs raised his head just long enough to say, "He's not sailed the Barbary with a Marchant like this before, Deth. He don't know what to look for. Look around — half the crew don't know, and half're happy as clams to be in it."

Avrel did just that, looked around and saw that many of the crew were as sullen and downcast as his mates, while others were grinning and chiding them for it. Still, the larger number was those who looked perplexed at the whole business.

Detheridge eased in her seat, though she still looked angry. "Aye, I'll allow that — so, you see, boy, it's —"

"Can we say?" Sween asked, cutting her off. "I mean, the contract —"

"The contract says we're not to talk about Marchant business off the ship," Grubbs said.

"Well, we're not off the bloody ship, are we, and he'll know soon enough."

Avrel just looked from one to the other as they spoke, becoming curiouser. He assumed they meant the contract they'd all signed to come aboard, which had provisions for keeping Marchant business private. None of them were to speak of it to anyone off the ship — not their cargoes, their destinations, nothing — on pain of their shares being forfeit, or even clawed back years later, after they were paid off. Those shares were why spacers sailed with Marchant, in large part, and why Marchant had so few spacers leave for greener pastures. A piddling percentage of each cargo, to be sure, but large in comparison to a spacer's wages — and paid only when each contract was up.

Subject to forfeit if a man didn't serve out his full term or, as Sween pointed out, if he violated any of the terms — discretion about Marchant business being foremost.

Avrel had paid little attention to that clause when signing aboard.

As I'll bring every bloody word of their business I may to Eades and hope he chokes them with it.

"So, what *is* the matter?" he asked. "And how can you be so sure, as Captain Morell's made no announcement about what's to come?"

"There's only one cargo needs compartments like that," Detheridge muttered.

Sween nodded.

"*Minorca's* going bloody slaver."

PART THREE

THREE

At first Avrel couldn't quite believe their revelation.

He'd heard that slavery was still practiced in the Barbary, of course, but hadn't really credited it. There were all sorts of stories about the Barbary, after all, just as there were all sorts of stories about some of the odder Fringe worlds — many might have a grain of truth, but were likely exaggerated for the most part.

Still, he couldn't quite see how it could go on here, surrounded as the area was by New London, the French Republic, *Hso-hsi*, and even Hanover — there were stories enough about the latter, too, but nothing to suggest they'd condone such a thing in what was, ostensibly, their own territory.

Then there was the economics of it. His own training at Lesser Sibward and aboard his family's ships had taught him what a powerful motivator money was, but also that there were some things there was no money in. Or little enough to make it not worth the trouble.

Just look at the shipping alone. For *Minorca* to fill her hold and sail across the Barbary, it'd be the same cost whether the cargo was men or machines — less, for the machines wouldn't have to be fed or guarded. He thought about the sheer logistics of having a hold full of people and balked at the cost. Machines could do any labor far more efficiently, so why bother with men?

He shook his head.

"This makes no sense," he said. "To what purpose? Machines to do virtually any work would be more cost effective and less trouble, even leaving off the risk of it becoming known."

His messmates were looking at him oddly.

"I mean, it's horrible, of course," he said, and felt that, but his first thoughts were to how this information could harm the Marchants and what use Eades could make of it. He wanted to be certain of the matter before rushing to message Eades, as well. "You're not speaking of indentures?"

The fringe worlds' indenture system might look like slavery to some, but it was really more of a debt system — and, except convicts or those taken up for debts already owed, it was voluntary. One sold several years of one's labor for the upfront cost of transport to a colony world in need of one's skills, or simply more population. It was no different than borrowing the money for property or an aircar, really.

"No, not indenture, boy," Detheridge said. "It's outright chattel for these folk."

"But ... why?"

"The Barbary's got worlds more isolated than the farthest Fringe planet," Sween said, and the others nodded. "Kuriyya was just the edge of it, close to others, even. Most of this space has so little to offer there're few who'll wish to go."

"And less to be brought back," Grubbs said. "Not much in the way of coin in the first place."

"A proper machine, for nearly any work, would take up less space in the hold than twice as many men," Avrel said. He still couldn't help but think they were wrong — or overreacting to something quite a bit more innocent than they described. "Where's the value in —"

"Some machine has the cost of a hundred men," Grubbs said,

"but one part breaks and there's a hundred men's labor gone." He shrugged. "One man breaks and there's still ninety-nine at the work."

Sween nodded. "Some company like Marchant comes in and they have the coin to do a thing right from the start, but a couple miners with a hard-scrabble claim far from it all?" He shrugged as well. "May not be the smartest, but it is what it is."

Detheridge glared at her plate and said, quietly, "Then there's the things men don't want no machine for."

Sween laid a hand on her shoulder, which surprised Avrel, as he'd never seen her take comfort from one of them like that, nor the others offer it.

"We'll hope it's none of that," Sween said.

Detheridge shook her head. "There's always some of that." She drained her mug. "I may be off next leave, lads."

Minorca was due to stay in orbit around Kuriyya until the work in the hold was complete, and then it'd been announced they'd have one more night's leave on the surface before she sailed. This had puzzled Avrel from the start, for it wasn't in any shipper's interest to stay idle around a planet longer than necessary. The work in the hold could have easily been completed while underway in *darkspace*.

"There's more than one won't come back," Grubbs agreed. "Lost shares or no."

Avrel frowned. "How does no one know about this? The government wouldn't stand for such a thing, Barbary or no. A New London flagged ship would never —" He broke off. There was nothing the Marchants wouldn't do, he suspected, if there was a farthing in it for them, and he well knew the influence they could place on those in government. Money talked in many places.

"Which of us'll speak out, even if we did run?" Detheridge asked. "You? Have you read your contract? Libel, slander, defamation, a slew of other things all come down to keep your bloody mouth shut or the Marchants'll ruin you — damages on top of they'll claw back every share you've ever been paid if you speak of company business. It means debt and indenture for your whole bloody family, just for the fees to defend the bloody case and never mind who wins. Who'll risk that?" She drained her mug. "Pay's good, though."

"Aye," the others agreed, but with dark looks. "There's that."

THE WORK on the hold finished, Morell announced, as Avrel's mates predicted, a further night's stay in orbit around Kuriyya and leave for all the crew. There were darker looks and fewer cheers than had greeted the leave granted when *Minorca* first arrived.

Avrel scanned the crowd when he exited *Minorca's* boat. For once, he wished to see some peddler-boy single him out with Eades' codeword, but there was none — only the same offers as when last they'd landed.

He caught sight of Kaycie at the boat's forward ramp, exiting with Morell and Turkington, but though she glared at him, he couldn't seem to catch her eye enough to indicate he must speak with her. Hard as it was to speak privately aboard ship, she seemed to be almost deliberately avoiding him these last few days — at least when she wasn't setting Hobler or his mates after him for some imagined slacking.

He'd given little thought to what might have got into her, though, as he pondered how to get a message to Eades. They'd not set up any sort of method for that, relying on Eades' network to contact Avrel instead. There'd been no indication until now that Avrel might have information on the Marchants that couldn't wait to be communicated — now, though, if Eades could get word of what Morell was up to to some authority, perhaps the Royal Navy, then *Minorca* could be found, stopped, and caught red-handed at something the Marchants wouldn't be able to buy their way out of.

There was his tablet, of course, which he could use to send a message, but that was tied to *Minorca* and his transmission would go first through her systems. He couldn't think of what he might send to relay the information that wouldn't give him away if it was monitored by Morell or Turkington — and he was certain all the crew's communications would be monitored now.

Nor could he encrypt a message, for that would be suspicious in and of itself.

There'd be little use in that, anyway, as any message he sent via *Minorca* would be weeks reaching Eades. It would be copied onto every outgoing ship bound in the direction of the message's destination, and copied from each of those to any others going the same way — whichever got there first would deliver it, and the process of marking it so and deleting all those copies would begin.

All of which meant *Minorca* would be done with her dirty business long before Eades was even aware of it.

No, he needed a faster method, and that meant a dedicated packet — or at least a fast one, bound in the direction of his message to begin with.

Those weren't cheap, though, and he had little coin — less than usual, truth be told, after his expenses of the previous leave. The house hadn't emptied his pockets entirely, but they'd taken more than the cost of the girl's hire for the trouble of getting him downstairs and parking him in the kitchen overnight. He'd not begrudged it at the time, but now he felt the need for every pence.

Not cheap, no, and neither were such things for hire in the common spacers' district.

They'd put down on Kuriyya at midmorning, leaving the crew with a full afternoon and night's leave, and Avrel's search took him well away from the pubs and brothels nearest the landing field, past the more genteel establishments catering to the ships' officers.

Here, though much the same services were on offer, the environment was more refined. There were no burly fellows or half-dressed girls hawking a place's wares on the street, no mugs sold through the pubs windows, and any advertising as to an establishment's purpose was quite a bit more subtle.

Avrel scanned the storefronts. A bank, he thought, or a gentleman's club, would either have what he needed or point him in the right direction — if they didn't throw him out before his first word. His ship's jumpsuit clearly didn't fit in with the attire on display in this district — even the rattiest captain at least gave the illusion of being a gentleman.

Then, his most creeping fear was realized, and he spotted Morell and Turkington, in conversation with another captain, coming his way.

If they saw him in this district, they'd wonder at it, and Avrel wanted no attention brought to himself at this time. He ducked quickly through the nearest doorway, hoping they'd not seen him and weren't bound for there themselves.

The door clicked shut behind him and Avrel had a moment to both bless and curse that the place he'd ducked into had no windows at all. Morell and Turkington wouldn't see him here, but neither could he be sure when they'd gone past. He'd have to count time in his head and make the best of it.

A clearing throat made him turn, and he took in the room for the first time. Dimly lit and well-appointed, it was a rather more upscale version of the place he'd spent his last leave.

I'm developing a disturbing habit of finding myself in brothels ...

The difference here, though, was that none of the girls appeared too enthused by his entrance. They all stared at him with varying degrees of distaste and hostility.

"Have you come to deliver a message?" an older woman, clearly the house's greeter, asked.

"Ah ..."

A large man stepped out of the shadows behind the woman, with a look for Avrel that was no friendlier than those of the women.

"Yes, now?" the woman asked. "If you've a message, tell me who it's for. We've not much custom this early and I'll not have you driving what there is away by hovering about."

"A message ... yes ... ah, for Captain Morell, of *Minorca*, if you please." Avrel squared his shoulders and tried to look confident, he needed just a few minutes' time for Morell and Turkington to pass by.

The woman frowned, then shook her head. "No — no Morell here. And none off any *Minorca*." She narrowed her eyes and the man behind her followed suit, as though their brows were connected. "You've a look about you — what are you up to? Whatever it is, I'll not have it in my house, you hear?" She said something to the man behind her in another language.

"Up to? No — I've a message. Is this the wrong house? Captain Morell said he'd be here, and —"

The brows narrowed further, and a second man stepped from behind the first, his brow mirroring the others. It was the size of the second man that made Avrel realize just how large the first was, as the second was ... quite large, but had been hidden all entire. Now all three brows advanced on Avrel.

"He's up to something," one of the watching women called out.

"He is," another agreed.

Damn me, but why'd it have to be a house? If there was one thing he'd learned watching his shipmates in port, it was that the ladies of a house could spot deception before it had its boots off.

"You leave," the bigger man said, as he stepped around the woman's left, his partner mirroring his motion to her right.

"I was just thinking that," Avrel muttered.

"Now," the smaller man said.

Avrel reached behind him for the door latch and backed away slowly.

"Yes, of course. I have the wrong place, I see. Different street entirely, is where I'm bound. I'll just —"

The men reached for him and Avrel felt a pain in his right ear as something grasped it. Which was quite odd, since the men hadn't reached him yet and he was backing toward the street.

The pain intensified as he was yanked backward through the doorway — a blessing as it got him out of the way of the two men and a curse as he was spun painfully around by the grip on his ear, then shoved to *thump* against the building's stone front.

He clapped one hand to his ear and the other to his chest where Kaycie had shoved him.

"Did you learn nothing from being carted back to *Minorca* like so much baggage?" she asked, glaring at him.

"I —"

"I thought better of you, Jon, I really did. Carousing like a common spacer!"

"But —"

"And as though you'd have coin enough to pay for such a place. Were you planning to run out on what you owed, as some of the men do?"

"Never! I wasn't —"

"Oh, tell me no stories. I heard you spin your tales for a dozen teachers, remember?" Her gaze darted to the doorway behind him, then down to the ground. "I suppose that's how you've spent these last three years, then? Running from one house to another, having your fill?"

"I never!" He flushed. "Well, I mean ... not so often as that." He hurried on as Kaycie's eyes flashed up to him again and she opened her mouth to speak. "I wasn't! Here, I mean." He held up a hand to forestall her. "Look, Kaycie, it's not like that. It's ... there's something coming aboard *Minorca* and I need to get word to Eades instanter."

"And your Mister Eades spends his time in bawdy houses, does he? Is that where you picked up the habit?"

Avrel'd had enough. He didn't like to see Kaycie upset, but this was beyond reason, and getting his message to Eades was too important for him to be delayed any longer. Besides which, what hold did she have on how he spent his time?

"Lord, Kaycie, I'd never taken you for such a prude. The Dark help your crews if this is how you'll set on them for a bit of sport!"

Now it was Kaycie's turn to flush. "I'd not!" Her gaze darted from Avrel to the doorway then back again. "It's only that —"

"And besides, what's happening aboard *Minorca* is more important. Look, we have to get word to Eades."

Kaycie frowned. "And what exactly is happening aboard *Minorca*? Captain Morell and Mister Turkington have been treating me quite oddly since I came aboard — as though my very presence were some great inconvenience. That's why I was following them."

"Following them?" Avrel only now glanced around and found that they were the focus of much attention on the street. No one was so close that they could hear much of what was said, but enough that he realized it was time to move along. Luckily there was no sign of Morell or Turkington, so they must have been far along before Kaycie dragged him out of the house. "Look, let's move this along elsewhere, shall we?"

KAYCIE LED him some distance away from the direction Morell and Turkington had been heading, then stopped in a less traveled part of the district.

"All right, then, what's this all about?" she asked. "You seem to know more about it than I do. What's got Captain Morell and Mister Turkington so unhappy with me?"

"It's likely they weren't expecting one of the officers to be replaced — not with what they have planned for this trip."

He went on to explain what Detheridge and the others had told him about the purpose of the compartments in the hold and his plan to get word to Eades.

Kaycie's expression grew more and more unhappy as he spoke, but she nodded along.

"It explains why they were unhappy with me from my very arrival," she said when he'd finished. "If they weren't expecting Mister Carr's emergency leave, then it must have come as an unpleasant shock. Likely they plan to inform me once we've set sail and present it as a *fait accompli*, much as they will to the crew —

93

those who don't already know." She nodded again. "Right. Your message is the best course, I think — let's be about it."

The day was wearing on with visits to four different banks before they finally admitted that the cost of a message with the priority they deemed suiting wasn't exaggerated by the first they'd spoken to.

"It's bloody usury," Avrel muttered as Kaycie swiped her tablet to transfer the funds. He glared at the banker, who was tapping his own tablet to acknowledge receipt. "It's a few bits of storage in the ship's core, we're not buying the bloody packet."

The cost had been more than both of them together had in coin, and more than Avrel had even in his accounts. It was only the luck of Kaycie joining up with him that allowed the message to be sent at all.

The banker shrugged, his full beard making his face unreadable, but his eyes showed amusement.

"The ship goes to where you wish first." He shrugged again. "For this, you pay."

Kaycie nodded and gave Avrel a little kick to the ankle. "Of course," she said, "and thank you."

She rose and gestured to Avrel. "Let's get back to the ship, Jon."

EVEN WITH THE message to Eades away, Avrel felt no better about things aboard *Minorca,* as there was no guarantee it would help.

Though he'd truly pinned all his hopes on it, the message would first have to make its way to Penduli, a long journey, despite having paid for it to be the packet's first stop, and then there was no surety Eades would still be there. If he were, some plan for intercepting *Minorca* would have to be arranged, and they'd been unable to so much as suggest where the ship might be bound. Neither he nor Kaycie had any idea, other than their eventual destination of *Hso-hsi,* where the ship's next stop might be.

Avrel had to resign himself to the likelihood that they wouldn't actually be able to stop *Minorca's* trading in slaves, only bear witness after the fact. At least he, and he was confident Kaycie, would do so, despite the risk of being sued by the Marchants. After all, Avrel had nothing more they could take from him and his only wish was to see the bastards torn down.

MINORCA SAILED with no more than one in five of her original crew left behind on Kuriyya.

Some of those might have honestly missed the ship's sailing, too drunk or otherwise occupied to note the time, but Captain Morell sent no quartermaster's mates to collect them. Most, given the grumblings Avrel heard, had left because they had no stomach for what was to come.

He noted that those who remained were nearly evenly divided on the matter, with a third seeming enthusiastic about their coming sail, a third angry, but not so angry as to give up their pay and shares in *Minorca's* journeys, and the last third seeming not to care one way or the other.

Of his mates, none stayed behind on Kuriyya, but none were happy about what was to come.

"It was an almost, I tell you," Detheridge muttered, as they settled in for the noon meal shortly after sailing. They were all sweat-soaked and tired from working the sails to tack their way out of Kuriyya's winds. She kept her voice low, so that those at the next mess tables couldn't hear, as the whole berthing deck was far quieter than usual, both from the missing crew and that none felt too jubilant. "There was a schooner out of Hanover taking on hands and offering fine rates."

"I'd not sail with the Hannies for any price," Grubbs muttered and spat to the side.

"Better than go a bloody slaver," Detheridge shot back.

"And you come back aboard, dint you?" Grubbs glared at her across the mess table.

"Only as I've a family to care for!"

Detheridge's voice was no longer kept low and they were drawing looks. Avrel and Sween glanced around, and Sween made a shushing motion with his hand, but the other two were having none of that.

"Oh, and my reasons are black as pitch, are they?" Grubbs rose from his seat, palms flat on the table and looming across. "While your family's all shiny? Will they stay so when it's this coin what puts bread in their craws?"

Detheridge rose as well, putting her face just centimeters from Grubbs' across the table.

"You leave my people out, Kalen Grubbs, or as the Dark's my witness I'll —"

Grubbs gave her no time to finish, instead he drove his right fist up from the table in a vicious arc into the bottom of Detheridge's jaw.

Detheridge was straightened and fairly lifted off the deck by the blow, knocked back to fall over her bench into the backs of the mess behind.

They straightened and turned, shouting, but took in the scene in a moment. Instead of anger, they grinned and steadied Detheridge on her feet. Those at the other mess tables stood as well, filling the narrow aisle between tables. There were shouts from farther forward and Avrel recognized both Bridgeford's and Hobler's voices, but the quartermaster and his mates were blocked, at least for a time, from making their way down the deck.

Detheridge shook her head, then shook off the hands of the men holding her up. She narrowed her eyes at Grubbs, spat to the side, then worked her mouth and spat again — this time something *clacked* against the deck where she spat, and she grinned.

Without a word, she lunged forward. Grubbs dodged the blow but not the grapple and found himself pulled forward, off balance, so that his face crashed into the table.

Detheridge stepped back and it was Grubbs' turn to shake his head and spit. Blood poured from his nose, which was skewed off-center.

Avrel and Sween stepped back from the two, merging with the crowd.

Grubbs and Detheridge glared at each other for a moment, then, as if they'd reached some unspoken agreement, lunged for each other simultaneously.

The crew devolved into shouts and cheers as the two pummeled each other, rolling about on the deck, then lurching to their feet and trading blows. Behind the first few rows of watchers, the crowd shifted and jostled to keep Bridgeford and his mates away as long as possible.

At first, Grubbs and Detheridge swung heavily at each other, but soon slowed as they tired.

The quartermaster's shouts grew louder as he and his mates forced their way through the crowd.

"Belay that, damn your eyes!" Bridgeford yelled as he shoved aside the last few watchers between him and the brawlers.

By this time, Grubbs and Detheridge were no longer so much fighting as aggressively hugging, neither one able to summon the energy to swing a solid blow and each using the other as means to stay on their feet. They clutched at each other and swayed a bit, as Bridgeford and Hobler sought to separate them.

"What's this? What's this about, then?" Bridgeford yelled.

Both of the fighters swayed on their feet, then, as one, hawked up blood and spat. It was possibly coincidence that each managed to do so close enough to spatter on Hobler's and Bridgeford's boots.

"*Damn* — off with you!" Bridgeford yelled, jerking Detheridge along with him. Hobler followed with Grubbs.

MINORCA LEFT the winds around Kuriyya and sailed on. Their destination wasn't announced and Avrel couldn't guess at it. He might have, if he'd had any duties on the quarterdeck and could track their position at all with a glance at the navigation plot. Still, he made a note of each sail change, the direction of the winds, the position of the ship's keel, planes, and rudder. It might be possible, given enough information, for Eades to narrow their destination.

When they finally did arrive, Avrel found his efforts were for naught, as they did not arrive at any system. Instead *Minorca* hove-to in the depths of the Dark.

There were two other ships, one a merchantman not too different than *Minorca* and the other a smaller, though better armed, sloop.

Avrel eyed the other ships as he tied off the last gasket holding *Minorca's* uncharged sails in place — he and Sween were the last ones done, as they had this side of the sail to themselves with Grubbs and Detheridge locked in the hold for fighting. Still, it gave Avrel more time to study the other ships.

Captain Morell had worked in close to the other merchantman, close enough for a boarding tube to be rigged between the two ships, and Avrel could make out every detail. He committed those details to memory, hoping it would allow Eades to track the other ship down, since they'd be unable to name the place of the meeting.

The sloop hung off in the distance, some thirty degrees above the two merchantmen and angled so that her guns bore on both ships. She was pierced for eighteen guns, Avrel noted. More than *Minorca*, though only half the size. She was clearly built for battle, not trade, and likely carried heavier guns than *Minorca* as well.

Neither ship had any identifying colors flashing from their mast or hull, and neither did *Minorca*.

A hand on his vacsuited shoulder drew Avrel's attention to Sween, who pointed down to the ship's hull.

Hobler was waving, the sign for them to make the last lines fast and return to the sail locker.

THE SCENE at the boarding tube was somber.

The last of the clasps were made fast by those still outside the hull and the tube aired. *Minorca's* crew gathered around the hatch. They had their instructions, but most were unhappy about the prospect now that it was here. It was one thing to ponder a thing in the abstract, while the figures of each man's share of a successful trading run were foremost — it was quite another to see the thing carried out.

"Not our place to judge what the Barbary's do to each other," Detheridge muttered. "This raiding back and forth, it's part of their culture, like, right?"

Grubbs nodded.

They'd been released from confinement and brought out to assist in transferring the cargo, as everyone aboard referred to what was about to be in *Minorca's* hold.

"Brought their ways with 'em, even from Earth, I think," Sween added.

The others, including those others of the crew close enough to hear, nodded agreement.

Avrel, who remembered his lessons from Lesser Sibward, knew better, but kept quiet. The others were trying to settle themselves to the task and wouldn't brook disagreement. While he knew that the Barbary might have been originally settled by those who could trace their Earth-ancestry back to that region on the planet — though they might never have actually lived there — the makeup had changed dramatically over the centuries. This region of space had become a catch-all for spacers and colonists not wanted elsewhere. The worst of the Core might make their way to the Fringe, but the worst of the Fringe made their way to the Barbary.

The hatch opened and two vacsuited figures entered. They scanned the assembled crew, then nodded to Captain Morell, who nodded back. Without a word being spoken, they made way at the hatch and other figures entered *Minorca*.

Unsuited, heads down, they shuffled forward, bound at wrists and ankles with thin cord, then bound together so that each one's hands were nearly touching the waist of the one in front.

Hobler counted them off as they entered, then cut the line attaching a group as he reached ten, the number to be placed in each of the hold's compartments.

"Harre," he said, "you and your mates take these."

The mess singled out kept their own eyes downcast, but Harre took the line and his mates surrounded the group to take them below.

So it went, each group of ten in the "cargo" being led below by one of *Minorca's* messes to be placed in a compartment.

The work went on in silence, save for Hobler calling out the mess which was to take the next group below, until one man in the shuffling line looked up at Hobler's voice.

"Oy! New Londoners? I'm Barden Dary off *Christina's Rose!* Bound home from *Hso-hsi* and taken off —"

One of the vacsuited figures from the other ship leapt forward and struck the man with a stunstick, knocking him to the deck unconscious.

"*No talk!*" the suit's external speakers sounded, and the figure waved his stunstick at the others.

Kaycie whispered something to Morell, who listened for a moment, then shook his head sharply. She stepped back from him, jaw clenched.

"Detail a mess to carry that man," Morell said, his own jaw tight. "And any man who speaks to the cargo will be put in-atmosphere at the next system, with no shares — is that understood?"

When only silence greeted him, Morell repeated. "*Is that understood?*"

The chorus of, "Aye, sir," was muted, but appeared to satisfy him.

"THIS AIN'T RIGHT," Grubbs muttered into his mug.

They were at their mess table, the berthing deck quieter than

Avrel had ever heard one. Captain Morell had ordered an extra issue of spirits, and so their mugs were full to brimming. Avrel sipped at his, wanting a clear head, while the others gulped, clearly trying to dull their wits after taking the cargo below — and the revelation that *Minorca* was not hauling only those taken in raids amongst the Barbary worlds, but spacers from New London and, he suspected, other nations as well.

Detheridge's face was the darkest, for at the end of the seeming never-ending chain of "cargo" had come two full compartments of women.

"Those girls were off *Völkerhausen*," she said, never taking her eyes from her mug. "I'll swear to it. They don't do that hair-beading nowhere else."

"Not no Barbary world, that," Grubbs muttered.

"It would be all right if they were?" Detheridge raised her eyes to glare at Grubbs. "Knowing what they're bound for?"

Grubbs looked up and the two locked eyes for a moment. They half rose, as though to launch themselves over the table once again.

Avrel leaned forward and laid a hand on each of their arms.

"Here, you two, that's enough." He pushed them back to their seats. "You're, neither of you, angry at each other, only at what *Minorca's* about. There's no defense of this, is there, Grubbs? And there's nothing right about it, nor anything to make it so."

Grubbs met his eye for a moment, then shook his head. "No. No, it ain't."

He and Detheridge sat back, returning to their silence while Avrel pondered their situation.

The cargo was all aboard, and *Minorca* set sail, with the other merchantman off in its own direction. He'd seen that while out on the hull making sail. He'd also seen that the second ship, the well-armed ship, kept pace with *Minorca*. Hanging off her stern like an escort.

Or a guard.

He was drawn from his thoughts by Captain Morell's arrival. The captain took his place at the fore of the berthing deck to speak,

Turkington at his side and Hobler with his mates between the officers and crew. Avrel noted Kaycie wasn't present, and wondered at that, before Morell began speaking.

"All right, lads," he said, "it's been a rough day, I know. There's none of us pleased by today's events, but we'll get through this as a crew, I assure you. Some of you have sailed through the Barbary before, some on Marchant ships — and you'll know that Marchant ships are the safest to make that journey on. There's no pirates in the Barbary who'll take on a Marchant hull.

"Well, that's not only for the Marchant's size and guns, you'll have realized now. There're deals to be made out here, and they're not all wholesome and clean, but it's what keeps our hulls and crews safe where others aren't. This trip is one of those — you make this sail, just a few more weeks, and you'll be keeping other Marchant crews, men and women you've sailed with before, free and clear in the Barbary, you hear?"

Morell cleared his throat.

"There's coin in it, too, for those of you who care — and that'll be most of you, I think, when the journey's done. When this cargo's off *Minorca* and we're on to *Hso-hsi*, the pay in your accounts'll taste just as good as any."

His face grew stern.

"But I'll have no complaints. This cargo's gone at our next stop and then we're done with it. I'll see any man who makes trouble before then put in-atmosphere — with no shares and no recommendation. Put out at our next stop, you hear?"

Avrel noted Grubbs blanch, as did no few others, as the implications of that sank in.

If their next stop was the destination for this cargo, then that would be no normal system. There'd be no legitimate merchantmen to take sail with after *Minorca*, even leaving aside the loss of, perhaps, years' worth of shares in previous voyages. There'd be no ship and little money for one of *Minorca's* crew put in-atmosphere at that port.

Morell cleared his throat again.

"You'll note Miss Overfield is not present," he went on. "She has taken exception to this voyage and our cargo. Exception which has gone beyond what I will tolerate." He took a deep breath. "My expectations for my officers are the same as for you, my crew. As such, Miss Overfield has been dismissed from the Marchant Company, she is confined to her quarters, and will be put in-atmosphere at our next destination."

THE SPOT GRUBBS had mentioned was well known to the crew. A squared-off area between the crates and vats of supplies that kept *Minorca* and her crew running for months in the Dark. The vats were tall and the crates stacked high, so that the light was dimmer inside the little area, about four meters on a side. One entered through either a narrow space between two vats, having to crawl at the middle, because the vats bulged out to meet there, or by sliding a crate, mysteriously left aboard an anti-grav pallet, aside to form a larger opening.

The latter had already been moved when Avrel arrived, slid back into the hold's main walkway.

Avrel made his way between the two crates to either side of the opening and was surprised, though he supposed he shouldn't have been, to find more than his messmates in the space.

There were six others there, standing or squatting with Detheridge, Grubbs, and Sween. Four women and two men, each from a different mess. A couple Avrel knew well, while a couple others he had only a passing acquaintance with, despite so long aboard ship together — those two were on the opposite watch and kept to themselves, in any case. The last two, Presgraves and Rosson, were two of the last Avrel'd expect to have come to this meeting, though.

Rosson was a hard man and didn't strike Avrel as the sort to worry all that much about where his coin came from. Presgraves was the same, but Avrel could understand her change of heart. The presence of so many women amongst the "cargo" had shaken more than a few of *Minorca's* crew from their apathy about this voyage.

He stopped in the entryway and raised his brows in query to his mates. Sween and Detheridge came over and they put their heads together so the others couldn't hear.

"Are you certain of them?" Avrel asked.

"They're all of like mind," Detheridge said, and Sween nodded agreement.

"And her?" Avrel nodded in Presgraves' direction. "Is she reliable? I mean, what with —"

"She's a good hand," Sween said. "I mean, sure, she's quick to fight a bloke ... and she's been up before the captain more than once for a roll in the hold, but that's only for the ship being so long a'space and she gets a bit ... twitchy, I guess."

"Twitchy?"

"The lass likes her sport." Sween shrugged. "And those charges on Pemsey weren't nothing — why, she's only to be gone from the system for six months and there's nothing more said about it."

"So, you vouch for her?"

Sween opened his mouth, then closed it and frowned. "Now, I wouldn't be going so far as *vouch*, now as I think on it, but —"

"She'll do for carrying word back to her mess," Detheridge said. "And that's all we're about just now, yes?"

"Yes," Avrel agreed. "All right, then." He stepped into the cleared space where the others waited. "So, you're all of like mind?"

"Aye," a few of them said, nodding.

"And our mates, as well," Presgraves said, "though we thought it best only one come from each for this."

Avrel nodded, suddenly wondering what, exactly, "this" was to be and how these newcomers and their mates had discovered that before he himself had.

He settled his back against one of the crates and looked at the others, who were all looking at him.

"What?"

Detheridge frowned. "This is all that's coming. Hadn't you best get started?"

Avrel frowned back. "What, me?"

NO MATTER that the others seemed ready enough to let Avrel "start", they weren't about to let him finish.

He'd no more laid out the bones of their complaint than they'd begun to flesh it out with plans. Presgraves' desire to blow *Minorca's* fusion plant as a last resort was not the maddest of the lot.

"Violence will get us nowhere," Avrel said. "Not with that sloop off our stern. She outguns *Minorca* in both numbers and weight, and likely out-mans us, as well."

"Well, there's no 'pretty, please, and may I' going to work with Morell on this," Presgraves said.

Avrel nodded, noting as well that none of those in the group had been referring to the captain as Captain or Captain Morell — no, it was "Morell" alone, and that spoke volumes of where their minds were. *Minorca* no longer had a captain that this group served.

"No, but it'll do us no good to ..." He trailed off, as none of them had yet really spoken the words — they'd danced around it, but not said it outright. He sighed. *Minorca* and his current situation were so far removed from what he'd thought his life would be years ago at school.

All those classes, but never a one on this.

He took a deep breath.

"It'll do us no good to take the ship —" He noted that more than one in the group winced as he spoke the words, knowing, as he did himself, that they, this group, were now fully liable to be hanged if they were ever found out. Even if they did nothing, he'd just spoken mutiny and they'd heard the words without dragging him to the captain immediately. Even Presgraves' talk of the fusion plant had been so couched in hyperbole that it could be argued as just malcontented talk. "No good at all to take the ship if we're then retaken by that sloop. We need to be patient and plan."

He met each of their eyes in turn. No one looked away from his gaze, but none seemed happy by where they were either.

Perhaps this wasn't the way, he wondered. Perhaps they should all just go back to their bunks and suffer through this voyage. He could jump ship at whatever system Kaycie was put off on and make his way with her —

A noise, barely audible, caught his attention and he was moving before he even thought.

He caught sight of the others' widened eyes as he spun and rushed between the crates that formed the entry way.

It was only as he caught sight of the figure in the hold's main aisle, crouched and peering around the crate's corner, that he realized he'd heard the shuffle of a boot against the deck. Only as he recognized Hobler, straightening now, face angry and mouth contorting to shout, that he realized they were found out.

Hobler stood, turning to shout for the guards near the slave compartments, and Avrel lunged.

He thought only to silence the man and gain a bit of time to think and talk to the others, but Hobler leaned away. The lean threw him off balance, his feet tangled, and Avrel's lunge to grapple and place a hand over his mouth turned into a shove.

Hobler was flung backward. His neck, just below his skull, hit the edge of the crate, as though Fate itself had stepped in to ensure the worst possible outcome.

There was a *thud* and a sickening *crack*.

Hobler collapsed to the deck, Avrel atop him.

Avrel knew in an instant that the man was dead. The feel of the body under him had lost all sense of humanity even before they'd come fully to rest.

He rolled off and scampered to the nearest crate, putting his back to it. His eyes were wide and he couldn't seem to get enough air. He hadn't meant to kill the man, only to stop him — silence him from yelling for a moment so that the guards wouldn't be alerted and they'd have a bit of time to think —

Detheridge and the others crowded into the hold's aisle. She looked from Avrel to Hobler's body, then back again.

"You were saying, lad?"

ONE DOESN'T EASILY COME BACK from death, no matter which side of the cause one's on.

Avrel was aware of his surroundings — the feel of a crate, solids for the carpenter's printer, he thought, at his back, Detheridge and the others crowding around, as well as their mutterings — but his focus was on Hobler. On the still, eerily still, body which used to be Hobler, at least.

"Oh, we're buggered now," Rosson muttered.

"They'll be on us," Presgraves agreed.

Avrel heard it, but couldn't quite process what they were saying.

It had all turned sideways in such an instant that he couldn't take it in. Until now, they'd just been talking. Oh, there'd been the intent to take the ship, but there was still that knowledge that they could walk away — go back to their berths and speak no more of it. There was an out.

No out now.

Hobler'd be discovered and someone would hang for it. Moreover, Avrel'd done it. He'd killed a man — all unintentional, perhaps, but still it was on him and no one else. He supposed there'd been that knowledge too, that no taking of *Minorca* could be entirely without violence, but that had been in the future. There'd been an out.

Someone else was speaking now, though in a calm, reasoned tone unlike the others.

"No, Presgraves, we've no need of you blowing the reactor. We're not nearly in straits so dire yet. Yes, should we need to, you'll have the job. For now, go with Detheridge, right? Detheridge, you take Presgraves to meet with her messmates — just the ones you're sure of, hear me, Presgraves? Get them down here. Sween, you go with Rosson and do the same. If there are others who'll join us — ones you're sure of, mind you— then bring them here. Or, better, if they're bright enough then just give them the eye and the nod with a whisper to be ready. Sure of, though, and I mean bet-your-mum's-life sure."

"Me mum's not so —"

"Not the time, Grubbs, you understand my meaning, I'm certain. Good. Now, Sween, you drag Hobler's body back into this hidey-hole and we'll set the crate in front. He'll be missed end of watch and that's but two bells from now. The ship's arms are under lock, so we'll need to free those in the slave compartments first and take the stunners from the guards, then we'll move on the quarterdeck and the fusion plant next, to ensure control of the ship — no, Presgraves, I'm afraid you'll be with me for the quarterdeck. If there's anything to be blown up, it'll go to you — my word on it.

"Detheridge, you take the fusion plant with two others while I take Sween and Presgraves for the quarterdeck. We'll each take however many of the captives might be trusted to follow instructions — I'll want no violence against the crew who're not immediately with us. They've not had a chance to change sides and I'll not hold inaction against them."

The speaker stopped and Avrel took his gaze from Hobler's body to scan the others, wondering what task he'd be assigned. The others stared back at him and he realized it had been him speaking all along, the years watching his father and other captains aboard family ships and the further years of training at Lesser Sibward coming to the fore when he most needed it.

"Well," Avrel said, "be about it."

The others moved off with more than one, "Aye, sir."

Detheridge held back a moment, staring at Avrel. "Knew you weren't just no bloody topman."

THE FOUR GUARDS outside the compartments holding the captives — even in the act of freeing them, Avrel had trouble thinking the vile word slavery — went down with nary a sound.

Avrel and Detheridge walked up to them, arguing loudly about which owed the other gulpers over some imagined bet, and grappled two, while Presgraves and Sween crept up from aft and drove the other two to the deck from behind. Once the scuffle started, the others, Grubbs, Rosson, and six more who'd responded to the call, swarmed out of the hold's shadows and took the lads down.

One of the guards, Lish, an able spacer from a world near the Barbary, offered to join in the mutiny, but Avrel wouldn't trust him to assist right off. He was put in a now empty compartment with the other guards and given the task of watching them.

"His world's been raided more than once," Detheridge said, "he'd likely help."

"I'll trust no one who wasn't with us to start this," Avrel said, "it takes but one shout to alert the quarterdeck we're coming and it'd be all over."

The quarterdeck and the fusion plant were the critical areas to take. If the latter wasn't taken, then power to the ship could be shut off and they'd have no choice to surrender — the former could lock down the ship, closing and fastening all of the hatches remotely, so that they'd not be able to make their way anywhere. They had to take both, take them cleanly, and at very nearly the same time.

"We'll take some of the captives, not too many and only those who know their way about a ship. Only those who look as though they'll follow orders and keep their heads about them. There's no one on *Minorca* responsible for their taking, and I'll have no bloodbaths of vengeance against our crew."

"Aye," Detheridge agreed.

They sorted things in quite a short time.

Avrel entered each compartment, told the captives what they

were about, asked who was a spacer, then picked the one or two who appeared not to be overcome with rage at their captivity. In the end, they'd added twelve men and women to their force. A large enough group to take the quarterdeck and fusion plant, with four stunners between them, but not so many as to draw too very much attention as they moved through the ship.

Up on the main deck, where the quarterdeck was located, Avrel paused. He checked his tablet to see the time. The other team would need a few more minutes to reach and take the fusion plant and engineering spaces — time Avrel decided to put to other uses.

"We'll free Kaycie first."

Sween gave him a puzzled look.

"Miss Overfield," Avrel explained, flushing at the further looks he got from both Sween and Presgraves. "She'll be of use taking the quarterdeck, as the hatch might open for her."

"Right," Sween said, though he looked dubious.

Avrel himself felt it was a slim chance, but Morell was not so punctilious about some things. It was possible, throwing an officer off the ship not being a thing he did all that often, that Morell'd simply had her locked up and not removed any of Kaycie's access to *Minorca*. If the quarterdeck hatch did open for her, it would save them the trouble of making some excuse to get through it. They could also, if *Minorca's* controls were similar to what Avrel'd learned at Lesser Sibward, throw open the hatches to the fusion plant, making things easier for Detheridge and her team.

"Kehoe's on her hatch, last I heard," Sween said. "Naught to do but keep her from talking to any of the crew, as I hear it."

Avrel nodded. Kaycie hadn't been aboard so long as to have any of the crew loyal to her — naught but himself, in any case — nor could she hope to escape to anywhere, so Morell must have thought there was little need for a tighter guard.

"Right," Avrel said. They were just down the companionway from the officers' cabins, tucked around the corner where the deck opened up to the main spaces. Kehoe and Kaycie's compartment were only a few meters away and there were only a few others of *Minorca's* crew about on the main deck. The ship would be on her current tack for hours yet, and the crew was resting and idle before being called to the sails once more. "We'll just walk up, casual-like, and distract him, then free Kaycie. Do you suppose there's a mess tray anywhere about? We could say we were delivering a meal or some —"

"Bugger that," Presgraves muttered. She stepped around Avrel and Sween into the companionway and strode toward the guard.

"Hell," Sween muttered.

"What's she —"

Avrel heard the sound of Presgraves' jumpsuit fastener coming undone and she shrugged as she walked so that it slid down her arms exposing her shoulders.

"Oy! Kehoe!" she called. "Fancy a poke before we're back at it?"

"You did say to distract him," Sween muttered, craning his neck to see around Avrel.

"*Hst!* He'll hear you and —"

"Mean to say, *I'm* distracted and I don't even get sight of the front bits —"

Presgraves was only a meter from the guard now, with her jumpsuit slid so far down her back that quite a bit of skin was exposed. Kehoe's view from the front would, indeed, have a few more bits in it.

Kehoe stared, open mouthed.

"Well?" Presgraves asked. "Quick, before we're called to change sail again, eh?"

"I —" Kehoe stared, swallowed, cleared his throat, and stared more. "Captain said I'm to guard this hatch, see? Next watch, maybe?"

There was silence for a moment, with both Presgraves and Kehoe standing still, Kehoe staring, then Presgraves leapt for him.

"*Next bloody watch?*"

Presgraves drove Kehoe to the deck with a flurry of blows. By the time Avrel and Sween rounded the corner, she had Kehoe on the deck, sitting atop him, with her arms wind milling furiously as she struck the man.

"I show you the *goods*, offer you a *poke*, an' you say, '*Next bloody watch?*'"

Avrel could hear Kehoe yelping, but the sound was overridden by Presgraves and the sound of fists hitting flesh. He and Sween each grasped one of Presgraves' arms, both struggling as she jerked against them to strike Kehoe again, and pulled her off. Avrel caught a glimpse of the "goods" as Sween then swung her around and backed her against the bulkhead.

"Here, now," Sween said, "no call to go and kill the bugger over it."

Presgraves stopped struggling and turned her attention to Sween, whose own attention was clearly on the goods.

"'No call?' No bloody call, you say?" Presgraves shrugged off Sween's grip, then grasped the goods and fairly shoved them in Sween's face, not to any obvious displeasure on Sween's part. "You'd tell these, 'Next bloody watch,' would you?"

"Not in life," Sween assured her, nodding in time to Presgraves' movements.

Avrel knelt next to Kehoe, who was bloodied about his nose and mouth and whose left eye was starting to swell.

"Are you all right, mate?"

"What ... what happened?" Kehoe shook his head. "'m supposed to guard the hatch."

"Ain't right, what he done," Presgraves said. "Ain't right, at all."

"What'd I do?"

"Get a girl all worked up thinkin' she'll get a poke, then tell her, 'Next bloody watch.'" Presgraves glared at Kehoe. "Not right, it ain't."

"What? I never —"

Sween kicked Kehoe's leg. "Shush, you bugger," he said, never taking his eyes from Presgraves. "No, not right at all, but, look here, you've your own work to be about, don't you?"

Presgraves turned her gaze to Sween, blinking. "What?"

"Well, now, what if we've need of the fusion plant blowing, eh? Where'll we be if you're off shagging and that needs done? Might have t'have someone else do it and you'd miss out."

Presgraves blinked again. "Right." She pulled her jumpsuit together and fastened it, to Sween's obvious disappointment, then frowned. "How about you, then? Blowing a thing up always does make me fancy a poke."

Sween cocked his head for a moment, then nodded slowly. "All right, lass — if we've need of your blowing the plant, I'm your man right after, right?"

Presgraves grinned. "There you go." She spat on Kehoe. "Not like this bugger, you."

"Whyn't you wait a bit down there, eh?"

Presgraves nodded and moved down the companionway closer to the quarterdeck, and farther from the fusion plant, much to Avrel's increased comfort. He and Sween shared a look.

Kehoe made to stand, but Avrel pushed him back down.

"Is she entirely right in the head?" he asked.

Sween glanced toward Presgraves as though to ensure she couldn't hear, then said, "No." He grinned. "But she's a fancy set of bits, if a man can keep the lass on track."

Avrel stood. "You stay there," he said as Kehoe started to rise too.

"But I'm to watch the hatch —"

"Stay put or I'll call Presgraves back and remind her of what you did."

"I'll stay right here then, shall I?" Kehoe lay back and closed his eyes. "Whatever you lot're about, I went down and out." His eyes scrunched tight. "Never heard nor seen nothing after, me."

"Good man."

Avrel rubbed his face. It was lucky so much of the crew was resting on the berthing deck, or this scuffle would have drawn attention. Even with it not, there was little time before Detheridge would be at the fusion plant, and the quarterdeck crew would need distracting when that happened. Still, he wanted Kaycie freed and with them, and if the hatch wasn't locked they still had time.

He keyed the hatch, which opened to reveal a darkened compartment. She must be sleeping, with little else to do while held captive.

Avrel stepped into the compartment, whispering so as not to startle her from sleep, "Kaycie, I've —"

Thump.

AVREL LOOKED up from the deck, wondering for a moment just how he'd got there.

Kaycie looked down at him, as did Sween and even Presgraves, who seemed to have come back from her place down the hall — Kehoe, he assumed, was still doing his best to appear incapacitated, especially with Presgraves back.

"Are y'with us, lad?" Sween asked.

"Jon, I'm so sorry." Kaycie tossed what she was holding — her compartment's small desk surface, Avrel saw, which had once folded down from bulkhead in one corner — onto her cot, but not before Avrel noted a smear of red on it. The compartment was lit now, which hadn't been the case when he entered, so he must have lost a bit of time.

Kaycie, with her desk ripped off the wall, waiting in a dark compartment, and now Avrel on the deck with, he noted, most of his face feeling a bit like Kehoe's must.

And bits of myself smeared on that desk panel. Right — that explains it, then.

Kaycie knelt and helped him sit up. He shook his head a bit to clear it, which was rather an error.

When his vision cleared, he grasped Kaycie's hand.

"I'm here to rescue you," Avrel said. "You hit me."

Kaycie flushed. "Right. Sorry about that. I thought you were the guard and I wanted loose."

"I'm here to rescue you," Avrel said. "You hit me."

Kaycie frowned. "Right, again. Are you —"

Avrel's senses were coming back a bit more and he struggled to his feet. "You hit me."

"I didn't know it was you!"

Avrel raised his hand to his face, probing at the tender spots. "You hit me hard!"

Kaycie stood, dropping Avrel back to the deck with another *thump*. "Well, it's no more than you deserved after ... after what you did on Kuriyya!"

Avrel blinked. What'd he done to Kaycie on Kuriyya? "What'd I bloody do to you?"

"Why you ..." She trailed off and clenched her jaw. "You're dense as any stone, Jon Bartlett!"

"We've little time for all this," Sween put in, "beggin' yer pardon for interrupting, miss." He frowned. "And why're you callin' him that?"

Kaycie flushed and cut her eyes from Sween to Avrel. "It's ... it's a name we use where I'm from." She narrowed her eyes at Avrel. "For a man who's a dolt and dullard."

Sween nodded. "Well, if yer through hitting him, we may be about the same sort of thing. As you seem to've been bent on gettin' yerself loose, and all."

"And what were you thinking to do once you were loose?" Avrel asked.

Kaycie shrugged. "I had no plan, but anything aboard *Minorca* would be better than being put in-atmosphere wherever we're bound. If the system is importing slaves, then I'd not hold out much for my chances there. I thought I might hide some message in the ship's mail core that could alert my family, or at the very least cause a bit of havoc and disrupt Morell's plans."

Presgraves nodded, grinning. "There's a plan, a bit of havoc." Her eyes widened. "Shall her and I off to the fusion plant, then?"

"No," Sween and Avrel said as one.

Avrel checked his tablet. "We've barely time to get to the quarter-deck," Avrel said. "Come on."

Presgraves pouted, but otherwise followed along.

THERE WAS no guard on the quarterdeck hatch. *Minorca* was no warship, after all. Morell must have felt he needed only to guard the captives and his one recalcitrant officer, while the rest of the crew was behind him.

Avrel knew differently. Many, perhaps most, of the crew were either ambivalent or opposed to *Minorca*'s nasty business. They might not assist his little group in taking the ship, but once that was done they'd not fight to free Morell, either — not once Avrel's lot were clearly in charge. As well, once in control of the quarterdeck, the fusion plant, and, he'd got the codes from Morell for the arms locker, the common crew would have no means to fight back.

He had only to gain that control, then announce his intentions to sail back to Penduli and the New London authorities, and most of the crew would at least play along, if not covertly support him.

"How do you plan to get through the hatch if he's keeping it locked?" Kaycie asked, as they made their way up the companionway. It was near the watch change and they could hear the bustling move-ment of bodies below on the berthing deck as those about to go on watch made ready.

"I'd thought to rush it when the watch changed," Avrel said. "There'll be new men for the consoles and he'll have to open for them."

Kaycie grunted. "Dicey."

"A bit." Avrel nodded. "But now you're with us, and there's a possibility he did no more than lock your cabin. Your tablet might still open the quarterdeck hatch."

"So, do we wait for the watch change or rush it now?" Sween asked.

"Wait, I think —" Avrel broke off as the hatch a deck below them sounded and footsteps came up the companionway.

All four of them turned to look as a spacer came into view.

"Blakesley," Sween said, nodding to the man.

"Sween," the man said, nodding to each of Avrel's group in turn. "Dansby, Presgraves ..." He frowned. "Miss Overfield? I thought you were —"

Kaycie smiled. "A misunderstanding — all cleared up. Are you going on watch?"

"Signals," Blakesley said. "Not much for it, with just the one ship along with us, but the station's got to be manned, don't it?"

"It does," Kaycie agreed. "Well, I have the next watch, as well, shall I walk with you?"

"Not but a few meters, but —"

"Fine, then." Kaycie slid the hatch open and gestured for Blakesley to precede her. As he passed, she plucked the stunner Avrel'd taken from the guards in the hold from where he held it behind his back out of Blakesley's sight. "You're from Thatchlow, are you not, Blakesley?"

"Aye, miss."

"My family's firm did some trading there, at times. It's known for its fishing, yes?"

Blakesley nodded, not noticing that Avrel and Sween were following along behind him, as well.

"Sport fishing, aye, miss. There's a beastie as shouldn't be missed, if such is your passion — horrible eating, but fights like a bugger ... begging your pardon, miss."

Whether to the presence of Blakesley's tablet or Kaycie's, Avrel couldn't tell, but the quarterdeck hatch slid open.

———

NO SOONER HAD the hatch slid open enough to fit her, did Kaycie shove Blakesley to the side and leap through.

Avrel followed immediately behind her, not entirely sure when or how she'd taken up the lead — not that she'd done it wrong, mind you, only that he'd been saying who was to do what since their meeting in the hold and now Kaycie was all but waggling her fingers for him to follow along.

Plucking that stunner from me, like she did and —

Through the hatch and onto the quarterdeck left him no more time to think.

Both Morell and Turkington were there, along with four spacers at the consoles — Turkington closest to the hatch and Morell on the far side of the circular navigation plot that filled the center of the compartment. All of them looked startled at Kaycie's appearance, then again as Avrel followed, and more so as Sween and Presgraves rushed in.

Kaycie raised the stunner and fired at Morell without a word, but the captain reacted before she could pull the trigger. Her shot went over his head, brushing the spacer at a console behind him and sending that poor sot to the deck in a crumpled heap.

"*Boarders!*" Turkington yelled.

It wasn't, strictly speaking, correct, as they'd been aboard the whole time, but it was what spacers were trained to react to. The quarterdeck crew was no different and, if they took a brief moment to determine it was Avrel's group Turkington was yelling about, they did figure it out.

Turkington grabbed Kaycie's arm and Jessup, the man Blakesley had been about to replace on the signals console, tackled Avrel at the knees.

"Get Morell!" Avrel yelled as he went down, slamming his fists into Jessup's back and kicking to try and break his grip.

Sween went around the navigation plot, but he was taken down by one of the quarterdeck crew and the two rolled about on the deck.

Presgraves took the clearer route to Captain Morell. She leapt onto the navigation plot, slid across the smooth surface, and off the far edge to land on the captain, who let out a grunt of pain audible even over the shouts and scuffles that filled the quarterdeck's space.

Avrel struggled to his feet, kicking at Jessup, who still clung to one of his legs. He grasped the edge of the navigation plot and pulled himself up, then ran his fingers over the surface. The menus were all much the same from ship to ship, and the Marchants could be trusted to keep their equipment updated, so there were no worries about it being antiquated. Neither Morell nor Turkington had the time to lock it for their entry, so there were no barriers to what Avrel planned.

Any ship traveling the Dark needed some means of controlling an unruly crew and *Minorca* was no different. Avrel flicked through the menus — Morell or Turkington would have known exactly where the setting was, but Avrel had to check all the possibilities, as well as kick and strike at Jessup to keep his footing.

He glanced up. On the other side of the navigation plot, both Morell and Presgraves had gained their feet, Presgraves between Morell and the plot.

"Step back from the plot, Dansby," Morell said, ignoring Presgraves. "Don't make this worse than —"

"Now, captain," Presgraves said, hands out to her sides as though to placate him. "Ain't none of us wants to —"

Morell's palm connected with Presgraves cheek in a loud *crack* that split the air of the quarterdeck. It stilled the ongoing struggles for a moment, as though it had been a gunshot. Even Jessup stopped struggling to pull Avrel down.

Presgraves straightened from where she'd been knocked aside by the blow, eyes narrow.

She stared at Morell for a moment, still and silent, then leapt for him, lips pulled back and fingers extended like claws.

"*You buggering bollocks washer!*"

Avrel's fingers found the setting he wanted and activated it. Throughout *Minorca*, hatches closed and locked themselves — he could only hope that Detheridge's group had made their way into the engineering spaces in time.

———

WITH THE SHIP sealed and none of the crew able to move from whatever compartment they were in, Avrel turned his attention to Jessup and the rest of the fights on the quarterdeck.

Most of which had ceased as the participants stared in awe or horror at Presgraves, who was on top of Morell and swinging blood covered fists at the captain's still form. She punctuated each blow with a shouted word and a grimace.

"*Don't! No! Man! Never!*"

Kaycie took the opportunity of Turkington's distraction to jab her stunner into his gut and pull the trigger. Turkington went down in a heap, and that — along with no little fear of Presgraves, Avrel was certain — took the fight out of the rest of the quarterdeck crew as well.

"Here, now," Sween called, easing toward Presgraves and Morell. He dodged a spatter of blood from one of her backswings and moved closer. "I think yer done there, girl."

Presgraves paused in her pummeling. She stared at Morell for a moment, as though evaluating her work, then nodded.

"Aye, he's killed."

Avrel couldn't see for certain, but took her word for it. He sighed. That would make things more complicated, and he wished it'd been avoided, but there was nothing for it now. They still had Turkington alive and he'd know of the slavery plans just as much as Morell, he was sure.

Sween offered Presgraves a hand up and she stood.

"Not certain you needed to kill him so bloody much," Sween muttered.

"Not needed? Did you see what he done?"

"Well, he shouldn't've hit you, sure, but —"

"*Hit me?*" Presgraves swung to face Sween, face twisted in fury. "That weren't no hit! The bugger *slapped* me, like I was some kind o' prissy tart!" She backed Sween up against the navigation plot, face close and one finger raised between them. "You mark me, Culloden Sween, and well. If ever you hit me, well, we'll have a proper go and then a pint and maybe a poke after, if you're still up to it — but, by the Dark, if ever you slaps me like I ain't worth your fist then ..." She stepped back and spat on Morell's body. "You hear me, Culloden Sween?"

"Aye. Aye, I do."

DETHERIDGE HAD TAKEN the fusion plant with nary a man lost on either side.

Of course, she didn't have Presgraves with her, so that was easier, Avrel thought.

With that, the quarterdeck, and the ship locked down, *Minorca* was theirs — now they simply needed to figure what they'd do with her.

Turkington, they locked in his cabin, after Avrel and Kaycie figured how to properly strip him of access to *Minorca's* systems. They'd not make the same mistake Morell had of thinking a locked hatch was enough and taking the rest for granted.

Kaycie stayed on the quarterdeck with Sween and Presgraves while Avrel went aft with the stunners. He, along with Detheridge and a few others, then went through the ship, releasing those of the crew they could rely on and herding any they couldn't below.

In the end, they'd replaced the captives in the hold with some half of *Minorca's* crew, and replaced the crew with a combination of captive spacers and those who'd never sailed before.

"Did you consider the sailing of the ship before you started this?" Kaycie asked Avrel when he returned to the quarterdeck.

"Not as such, no." He paused. "Did you consider anything past

121

getting out of your cabin when you ripped the desk from the wall and beat me with it?"

Kaycie flushed. "Not as such."

"There you are, then."

Avrel thought they weren't really so bad off, nearly half of *Minorca's* crew was still free. He was a bit concerned about some of them, but they were not so many as could retake the ship — not now that the whole of the crew was aware and on the lookout for such a thing. Many of the released captives were quite experienced spacers, if they were to be believed, and he had no reason not to.

"We should be all right," he said. "Not all of the spacers in the hold were New Londoners, though, so there's a bit of a language problem below."

Merchantmen, and even some navies, had eclectic crews to begin with, picking up hands in whatever port and from whatever system they were available. What they had now, though, was quite a bit different than a few hands who'd signed on in some past port. They had Hanoverese, French, *Hso-hsi*, and hands from even farther away than that. There was even one lad who claimed he was from some system off on the far side of Earth itself, and how he'd got clear around the massive globe of explored space only to be captured by some pirate in the Barbary, Avrel couldn't fathom.

"Detheridge feels we'll get by well enough, though," Avrel said.

"So, what do we do now?"

Avrel paused — he'd truly not thought too very much beyond taking *Minorca* than Kaycie had getting out of her compartment. He'd thought only to put a stop to the ship getting any closer to offloading their human cargo.

"Well, we're a fine pair of mutineers, aren't we?"

Avrel winced. Kaycie's words struck home and he'd not cared to think of himself as that, even since they'd taken *Minorca*.

He took a deep breath. They'd not be branded as that, not when the whole story was told, at least.

"Next is we need a way to lose our friend there," he said, nodding to the navigation plot. Their escort was still in place, sailing placidly along aft and a few points off *Minorca's* stern. "Do you have any thoughts?"

Kaycie shook her head. "My family's policy was always to flee, then surrender in the face of a fight. The best chance of survival with pirates is always not to anger them — being left off in a ship's boat or on some remote world's always preferable to what they'll do if one of them's killed."

Avrel nodded. It was his own family's policy as well, and what was taught at Lesser Sibward. One might flee and have a chance of escape, but if it came to shooting a pirate's ship would usually outgun and certainly outman a merchant. If one couldn't get away clean it was better to give in — the pirates wanted the cargoes, after all, and not the crews. Sometimes not the ships themselves, even.

"I doubt that will work here."

"No," Kaycie agreed. "But it doesn't change that we're outgunned and outmanned. We'll need something cleverer." She grinned at him. "So, what's the plan, Jon?"

"DOUSE THE SAILS AND HULL," Avrel ordered.

"Aye," Grubbs said.

Grubbs was at the quarterdeck's signals console. He and Privitt, a man from Rosson's mess, at the tactical console, were the only ones manning the quarterdeck other than Avrel. Everyone else, those who could be trusted, at least, were either on the few guns *Minorca* carried or ready at the boarding tubes. They all had their vacsuits on, as did the rest of the crew, and those of the captives not huddled away in the hold for protection.

At Avrel's order, *Minorca's* sails went dark, no longer charged by the powerful particle projectors that let them harness the *darkspace* winds. Her hull, as well, went dark, and the ship began to slow, no longer propelled against the resistance of the dark matter that permeated the space around her. To an external observer, she'd appear dead and lifeless.

"Detheridge's ready," Grubbs said.

Avrel nodded, eyes on the navigation plot.

How long should it take? Time enough to run through diagnostics, he supposed. He ran fingers over the plot, plying the menus.

"A call to the engineer to find out what's the trouble," he muttered. "No, a runner — and we'd have no diagnostics on the quarterdeck. These consoles would be dark, wouldn't they?"

"Never been aboard a ship with the plant shutdown before," Grubbs said.

Most spacers hadn't, Avrel knew. It was a possibility, but rare. If the plant detected a problem, it would shut down, for the alternative would be far worse. The ship would be without power for any but emergency systems — until the plant was ensured safe and could be restarted.

"Yes, a runner to the plant," Avrel said aloud, "then time for him to return with a message. A few minutes at least, and Captain Morell would be far more concerned with the workings of his ship than our escort there."

He drummed his fingers on the plot, waiting. The other ship had noted *Minorca's* plight now, and there was a flurry of activity on her hull. Sails trimmed and their charge lessened to slow her, and she was coming up into the wind herself to slow further. She'd already sailed past *Minorca* as the darkened, apparently powerless, ship slowed to a stop.

"All sorts of signals," Grubbs said.

Avrel could see that on the plot, the image of the other ship brought inboard by passive optics and displayed there. Her masts and hull were flashing brightly, demanding a response from *Minorca*.

"Detheridge —"

"Keep her inboard," Avrel said. "We're scurrying about with our own troubles right now. We're a Marchant ship, as well — we'll get around to answering in our own bloody time, won't we?" He stared at the other ship's image, wondering what that captain was thinking. "Time enough for an answer from the engineer, and a bit of a whinge about why is this happening to me, I suppose." He took a deep breath. "Time to realize we're in a fix and more time to accept that a bit of help won't go amiss."

A fusion plant restart could be done alone, but it would tax the ship's batteries to their limits — wear that had a cost, and they'd need replacing sooner. An expense like that, coming off a voyage's profits — well, what captain wouldn't want to avoid that?

Better to string a cable from another ship if one was lucky enough to have another nearby.

"Send her out."

"Aye."

The sail locker's hatch in *Minorca's* bow cycled slowly and a single, vacsuited figure emerged.

Detheridge made her way a bit to the starboard side, where the other ship now lay off *Minorca's* bow, having sailed past, then come up into the wind to stop.

Detheridge raised her arms and lit the long lighted sticks she held, beginning the long, laborious process of spelling out their message.

Fusion SCRAM. No Power. Assist - interrogative.

Detheridge was playing the part of *Minorca's* quartermaster, arranging things while the ship's officers dealt with what was certainly a mess inside the hull. She finally arranged things to everyone's liking and the other ship took up moving again — it was on them to make the docking, with *Minorca* ostensibly unable to move.

The other ship charged her sails, pulled them around to fall off the wind and sail away downwind, then circled back to come at *Minorca* from behind. It would be an awkward docking as *Minorca* had been on the port tack when her sails went dark, leaving her in the same attitude toward the winds, rather than coming up into them to heave-to as was typically done. The other ship would have to come alongside while on the port tack as well, a more difficult maneuver.

They managed it, though, and came to rest a few dozen meters from *Minorca's* starboard side.

The boarding tube extended, touching *Minorca's* side with a crew of vacsuited figures carrying a thick cable already inside it. They'd left the outer hatch to their own lock open and Avrel hoped Kaycie, on the berthing deck with their few guns, had the sense to target both those in the tube and that lighter, inner hatch. He swallowed heavily at the thought, but if they could expose the other ship's interior to vacuum quickly — well, the crew likely wasn't suited, there being no reason to expect *Minorca* to attack, after all.

Avrel clenched his jaw.

"Fire."

THE ACTION WAS short and brutal.

The other crew, all unsuspecting, was indeed unsuited. Avrel would never know how many died when *Minorca's* first broadside opened her main deck to vacuum.

The other captain and his crew weren't fools, though, and *Minorca's* guns weren't nearly enough to settle the matter in one go.

It was barely two minutes, not long enough for any but one of *Minorca's* guns to reload, before the enemy's gunports opened. They'd not bothered to rig their own gallenium nets to keep the *darkspace* radiations out for a time, simply flung the ports open and stuck the crystalline tubes of their guns through to fire into *Minorca*.

The boarding tube and its inhabitants had been shredded by grapeshot, canisters that split the thick lasers of the main guns into dozens of thinner beams, as Kaycie had indeed targeted them. Those in the tube, men who'd only been coming to assist a ship they thought was in trouble, were slaughtered in the one blast, but the tube itself remained in place. Open to vacuum, but still usable to propel oneself between the ships. The lock on the other side was open to space, blasted apart in their first salvo, and Avrel's crew was already suited, as the enemy was not.

Figures streamed across from ship to ship, even as the guns were reloaded and fired again. One or two were struck with the full force of shot, but the others kept on. Kaycie had organized the boarding party from the former captives, and they knew the stakes — it was take the other ship, die in the attempt, or return to their captivity.

They'd opened *Minorca's* paltry armory and handed out the weapons — bladed mostly, with the few chemical projectile sidearms going to those spacers who claimed some proficiency with them. Firing those in vacuum, especially if a ship were to lose its gravity generators, wasn't something most merchant spacers practiced at.

The guns on both ships were firing again, erratically as the gun crews heaved shot into the breaches. The heavy canisters made up of capacitors to hold the charge and lasing tubes that fired through the guns' barrels were encased in gallenium to protect them from the *darkspace* radiations that made all electronics useless when exposed.

"Bugger it," Avrel muttered. He clamped his vacsuit helmet over his head and gestured to the others. "There's nothing to be done from the quarterdeck, lads — it's not as though we're going anywhere."

Grubbs and Privitt clamped their own helmets on, grasped their weapons and followed.

Avrel made his way down to the gun deck. He spared a brief nod to Kaycie, who was rushing from gun to gun, encouraging their crews and seeing to their aim. He wished that he could take the time to say something to her before joining the fight on the other ship, but with the radiations inboard the suit radios were down and he didn't think he should take the time to touch his helmet to hers so she could hear.

Instead he raised a hand, turned that into a sweeping gesture forward, and flung himself through the tube at the other ship.

———

THE AFTERMATH of the battle shook Avrel to the core.

No class at Lesser Sibward, nor his travels aboard ships, had prepared him for the bleeding, burned, and broken bodies littering the decks of both *Minorca* and *Fancy*.

It was odd, he thought, that he didn't remember much of the battle itself, though. Only images of his blade and the blades of others — blocked or swinging or cutting through a vacsuited limb.

His first thoughts were of Kaycie, and though she'd been the one to send word that *Fancy's* captain had surrendered and the ship was theirs, Avrel wouldn't be satisfied until he'd gone through the boarding tube himself and seen her whole.

She'd already seen to securing *Fancy's* crew and officers, so then came the task of sorting the wounded and seeing to their treatment. The worst seen to wherever they lay and moved to a makeshift sick berth in *Minorca's* hold, for the main sick berth couldn't hold so many. Of those not in dire straits, *Fancy's* crew were sent to their fellows in that ship's hold, to be treated as well as could be, while the *Minorcans* saw to their own.

Detheridge had taken a slash to her belly during the boarding, but her vacsuit had sealed and *Minorca's* surgeon was confident in her recovery. Grubbs had been less lucky as a bolt from *Fancy's* guns had taken off his left arm at the elbow. Avrel stopped to visit them both, as they were resting side by side, and was surprised to find them in good spirits.

"Oh, a prosth'll set me right, once we're somewheres civilized," Grubbs said. "No worries."

Detheridge simply nodded and smiled, her expression making Avrel wonder if the surgeon hadn't given her a bit much in the way of painkillers.

Regardless, he clapped them each on the shoulder and moved on to have a word with each of the other wounded.

Once that was done, and both ships put to rights so that they could sail again, it was time to decide on their next move.

Minorca's crew and the captives were divided in their desires. Some, those who'd not participated in the taking of the ship, wanted off as soon as possible. They wished nothing more to do with the mutiny, nor with standing against the Marchant Company, and Avrel couldn't blame them — they'd not asked to be put in a place to take such a stand, merely wanting to live out their lives and do the work they were suited to. Others — Barden Dary and his fellows who'd come aboard as captives — wished to sail off and make their own way in the Barbary. Avrel suspected their own way might have something less than honest trading to it, but couldn't blame them either, not after their experience. Some of *Minorca's* crew fell into this lot as well. The minority were those who, like Avrel and Kaycie, felt the need to sail back to New London space and spread the word about the Marchant's actions.

In the end, nearly everyone got their way.

Dary and those who wished to sail with him took *Fancy* and disappeared into the Dark, while Avrel took those who wished to find other berths to Kuriyya and set them in-atmosphere. They'd have the chance, at least, to find berths on honest merchantmen and leave their time with the Marchants behind them. Some might contact the company and try to reestablish themselves, but Avrel thought that a losing proposition for them. He doubted the company would have anything to do with any of *Minorca's* complement again. Avrel, Kaycie, and those others who wished to tell their story set sail in *Minorca* — undermanned, but willing — for Penduli.

Avrel kept *Minorca* in orbit around Kuriyya for three weeks, making the final repairs for the long haul back to Penduli. It gave the crew, those who were left, time to think about whether they truly wished to return to New London space with *Minorca*. Some few more decided it wasn't truly in their best interests to do so.

Avrel, on *Minorca's* quarterdeck, sighed as the ship's boat returned from the surface for the last time, three more short than it'd landed with. He tried hard not to begrudge them their decision, but it was hard when he had but two short watches aboard. The sail back home would be grueling for all of them.

He stepped to the navigation plot, scanned the shipping to ensure no one else was about to leave orbit, and nodded. It was time.

"Signal our intent to break orbit, Grubbs," he said. He'd put the one-armed spacer on the signals console, as he needed every able-bodied man for *Minorca's* sails. Grubbs was showing some aptitude for it, as well, and it would do the man no harm to add that to his resume for future ships. He might decide not to return to the tops, even once he had a prosthetic for his missing arm.

"Aye, sir."

Kaycie stepped up to the navigation console beside him and laid a hand over his.

"And next?" she asked.

"Home. Home and make the bloody Marchants pay."

EPILOGUE

Minorca's speakers chimed once, marking half an hour into the morning watch. The quarterdeck was peaceful, as was the rest of the ship, with none of the bustle normally associated with the morning. None of the crew felt any particular need to clean or perform the small bits of maintenance typically done at the start of the morning while their breakfast was cooking.

Avrel supposed he might have some of the crew who'd stayed loyal to Morell do the cleaning, but they were nearing Penduli — just a few days away, if the navigation plot were to be believed — and why should he take the risk? Besides that, once at Penduli they'd be turning the ship over to the authorities and likely never see her again.

Perhaps at trial ... perhaps they'll ask to tour the hold where the spacers were kept on their way to whatever fate was in store for them.

Or perhaps not.

Avrel wasn't entirely sure what to expect once they arrived at Penduli. *Minorca's* officers would be tried, of course, but would the case ultimately be heard there or would it be moved coreward, perhaps to New London itself, in order to charge and bring others in the Marchant Company to justice?

His lips quirked up in a grin.

Either way, once word was out, Marchant would be badly hurt, perhaps even destroyed.

His grin widened as he thought about the headlines.

Marchant Company Stock Plummets, he thought. *Frederick Marchant Brought Before the Dock. Slavers in our Midst!*

The press would have at the Marchants like spacers on the last pint, and the public cheer them on. There was nothing either liked more than a man-makes-good story, save a man-makes-good-and-now-it's-bloody-time-to-tear-him-down one.

"Sail!"

"Where away, Grubbs?" Avrel asked.

"To port, up fifteen," Grubbs answered. "She's small — single-masted. Looks to have just come about and is making toward us — she likely saw us before we saw her."

Avrel nodded. *Minorca's* greater expanse of sail, and he had all she'd bear bent on now in his eagerness to make Penduli, would make her visible at a greater distance than smaller ships. They were close enough to Penduli, though, that this might be some revenue cutter set on inspection.

"Keep a close eye on her for signals, Grubbs. If she's Navy I'll wish us to respond to her instanter, you understand?"

"Aye."

Avrel nodded. Their initial greeting, whether in *darkspace* or on arrival at Penduli, would likely be a bit tense — until the facts were out about *Minorca's* business. He wanted nothing to make the authorities tenser than they may be after whatever rumors of what had occurred about *Minorca* in the Barbary made their way back.

"She's signaling."

"What message?" Avrel frowned and glanced at the plot. The other ship was still quite distant, just at the most distant range she might hope for signals to be visible.

"*Heave-to,*" Grubbs said after a moment. To his credit, the one-armed spacer had taken to his new post with a vengeance, studying signals and the workings of his console. He could often be found off-watch holed up with his tablet and Detheridge in some remote, private corner of the hold.

Studying, Avrel considered with a half-hidden grin. But, for whatever else the two might be up to, Grubbs had learned his signals well. *A revenue cutter, then — and bored, if she's signaling so early. Wants to take no chance we'll sail on before she has a look at us.*

"There's some more," Grubbs said. "So dim from the distance the computer's having trouble with it, but I think she's spelling out ..." He squinted at the blurry image of the ship, fuzzy lights flashing in sequence. "Y ... o ... u ... b ... l ... o ... o ... d ... y ... f ... o ... o ... l ... p ... e ... a ... r ..." He looked to Avrel, brow furrowed. "Then it's *Heave-to* again — and they've added *Imperative*."

Avrel sighed.

"That'll be for me, then."

"YOU FOOL! YOU INSUFFERABLE, BLOODY *FOOL!*"

Eades was in a state.

No sooner had *Minorca's* hatch opened to the docking tube strung between her and the other ship, than Eades himself was through it. Avrel was a bit surprised at the skill with which the man grabbed the tube's end and swung himself lithely from the tube to the artificial gravity within *Minorca's* hull — all the while keeping on with a non-stop commentary on Avrel's actions.

"Mutton-headed, bespawling, addlepated *dalcop!*" Eades went on as Avrel ushered him in to *Minorca's* master's cabin and slid the hatch shut.

Kaycie was staring at the man, her eyes wide with astonishment, but a growing grin.

"Old friend, Jon?" she asked. "Appears to know you well."

"And you're no better, Miss Overfield, to have participated in his lunatic endeavor."

Kaycie's brows rose further at this, likely in surprise that this stranger so easily identified her.

"Who —"

"I'd have thought you had better sense, by all reports," Eades went on, "but I can see where any time around *this one* would make anyone into an equally blithering idiot."

Avrel assumed he was Eades' "this one".

"Who exactly is this, Jon?" Kaycie's tone had grown cold and Avrel hurried to usher the two to seats on opposite sides of the late Morell's dining table. "And what does he mean by —"

"Let's all sit for a moment, perhaps have a drink, shall we?" Avrel looked around, but had no idea where Morell's stores were kept. He'd avoided making use of the master's cabin, even after taking command of *Minorca*, as it hadn't seemed quite right to take on the dead man's possessions. He moved toward the hatchway. "I'll send a man for a bit of beer, perhaps, and —"

"There's drink in that cabinet," Eades said, pointing. "And lord knows I need one."

Avrel stared at him for a moment, torn between relief that the commentary on his intelligence had ended and bewilderment at how Eades would know where Captain Morell kept his stores. He went to the indicated cabinet, opened it, and found an array of bottles — spirits on the bottom and a rack of wine

"Those are the ones he'd not trust his steward with," Eades went on. "Bring back several and let's get on with this."

"Jon —" Kaycie began.

"Malcome Eades, Foreign Office," Eades interrupted. "I know you because I'm the one who arranged for you to be aboard this ship, thinking — a now pointless exercise where you two are at work, I see — that you might be a sort of mitigating influence on young Mister Bartlett's less endearing qualities." He fixed Avrel with a cold gaze. "By which, I mean the whole of him, I assure you."

"Now see here —"

Avrel set two bottles on the table with a loud *thump*.

"Oh, let him talk, Kaycie. He'll eventually tire of showing off his own cleverness and get to business." He poured. A spiced rum he'd not have thought to Morell's liking, and he hoped not to Eades' either, then set glasses beside the other two before taking up his own. "Mister Eades," he said, raising his glass. "My apologies for whatever it is I've done to muck up your, I'm certain, cleverest of plans. Please, do, explain your brilliance, my own stupidity, and how it is you shall go about fixing it now."

Eades' eyes narrowed, but before he could speak Kaycie placed her palms on the table and half rose, leaning over and fixing her gaze on each of them in turn.

"Gentlemen, though I do await an explanation I'm certain will be both edifying and —" She turned to Eades. "— admirable in its form, if ever either of you interrupts me again, I'll box your ears bloody!"

Avrel had to chuckle. He'd never heard Kaycie curse before, and for her to get it so wrong relieved a bit of the tension he was feeling.

"If you're going to curse, you should get it right," he said. "The 'bloody' goes before 'ear', there, so it'd be —"

"I don't curse," Kaycie said, quietly. *Too quietly*, sprang to Avrel's mind. "And I spoke my meaning precisely, have no doubt."

"Oh —"

Avrel's hand went reflexively to his ear and he noted Eades' fingers twitch as though to do the same.

Kaycie stared at them for a moment, then, with a satisfied look, sat and raised her own glass.

"Now, Mister ... Eades, was it? Yes? Will you be so kind as to *explain* what it is we've done that's upset you so?"

Eades' lips curved and he fixed his eyes on Kaycie, then gave Avrel a quick glance.

"Yes," he said, "I shall. The two of you, you see, have shattered any hope of using *Minorca's* actions against the Marchant Company. I needed *information*, boy, not this ... fiasco."

Avrel pondered this for a moment. He'd suspected there was some difficulty due to Eades' distress, but couldn't for the life of him figure what it might be. They had the ship, the ship's officers, and some of the crew as those complicit in the transport of the slaves, added to his own and Kaycie's testimony and that of the freed spacers themselves.

"We've witnesses a'plenty aboard," he protested, "and all but Captain Morell of the officers and ratings. I don't see what the trouble is."

"Neither do I," Kaycie added. "It all seems nicely wrapped to me. Just a matter of telling our stories."

"Your stories, yes. You don't see it at all ... no, you don't." Eades sighed. "You're both a bit young to understand how the universe actually works, I suppose." He held up a hand to forestall their protests. "Let us say, then, that you sail *Minorca* into Penduli as you intend. Rush to the station master, I suppose, or did you plan on going straight to the Naval offices and the port admiral?" He shook his head. "No matter.

"Once the matter's brought to the authorities, two things will happen. First, you two and all those you don't have locked up will be charged with mutiny." He held up his hand again at their protests, adding a "tut" sound to emphasize it, which drew narrowed eyes from Kaycie. "Charges *will* be brought. You did, after all, take the ship from her rightful captain, there can be no doubt of that, and, yes, there may be some justification to it, but that will be a matter for the court to decide, do you see?"

Avrel nodded and, after a moment, so did Kaycie. He did see that. A ship whose captain had been deposed would see the crew tried for mutiny, no matter the circumstances — those charges might not result in conviction, depending on the circumstances, but there'd be charges nonetheless.

Eades appeared satisfied that they understood that, at least.

"And so," he continued, "this will now become the testimony of accused mutineers against their former captain and officers. Mutineers and *pirates*, as those who weren't properly part of *Minorca's* crew will be charged with piracy."

Avrel realized Eades was talking about the rescued spacers, and moved to object, but Kaycie was nodding.

"Yes," she said, "there will be charges, won't there ... as many as can be thought of."

"Ah," Eades said with a sad smile. "Miss Overfield is not, perhaps, so naive as I thought the both of you were."

"But —"

"The courts work for Marchant, Jon," Kaycie said softly. "We've both seen that, haven't we? Whether directly bought or only because the laws favor the powerful by nature ... they work toward Marchant's interests and those interests are for all those who took *Minorca* to be painted black as pitch." She nodded to Eades. "The station master?"

"A lovely vacation home in Penduli's Lakes District. Far beyond his means, I'm given to understand."

Kaycie nodded. "And the port admiral?"

"Admiral Fitzsimon Ashwill. Strong Naval ties in that family ... those not in merchant service, that is."

"I see. Merchant service with ..."

"Exactly."

"They're everywhere, aren't they?" Kaycie asked.

Eades sat back in his chair and sighed. "Indeed."

"But the Marchants are in the slave trade," Avrel protested. "When that comes out —"

"How will it come out?" Eades asked.

Avrel saw that Kaycie was nodding along with Eades, but didn't see it himself. What did they understand that he didn't? "We've a shipload of spacers who'll bloody shout it to all who'll listen!"

"What is it you see that our young friend does not, Miss Overfield?"

Kaycie closed her eyes as though pained. "Morell."

Eades nodded.

"Yes," Avrel agreed. "He commanded *Minorca*, took on the cargo of slaves, transported them, and he works for the Marchants. It's their ship! He was their man!"

"Morell is dead." Eades said flatly. "And the Marchants, as they have in the past, will claim he was simply a rogue captain." Eades' voice took on a tone of righteous indignation. "'We cannot police every action of every captain of every ship,' they will say ... again. 'Were Captain Morell alive, he would be dismissed from our service forthwith and his pension forfeit, as an example to all our captains that actions outside the kingdom's laws will in no way be tolerated.'" Eades shrugged. "That is the arrangement, I'm sure, between these captains and the Company. Follow orders and you will grow wealthy, disavowal if you are caught. And some promise of wealth or threat to their loved ones to maintain their silence, certainly."

Avrel thought he caught a note of recitation in Eades' tone as well, as though the words had been heard by him far more than once.

"The Marchant Company has an extraordinary number of rogue captains, you see. Had Morell been taken alive, he might have some evidence, some instruction, which could implicate those higher up in the Company."

"But —"

Kaycie drained her glass. "The best we could hope for is that Morell alone would be condemned as a slaver, the worst would be that we ourselves are convicted of mutiny. And Morell is beyond justice now."

Eades nodded. Avrel almost thought his face held some sympathy.

"There is, I'm afraid, no benefit at all to your returning to a New London system. No benefit at all, and far too great a risk, I'm afraid."

Avrel struggled to understand. He'd been prepared for a triumphant return — rescued spacers and evidence against the Marchant's foul deeds. Now it was all crashing down.

"This can't be," he whispered.

Both Eades and Kaycie were silent, as though giving him time to accept what they already understood.

"What do we do, then?" he asked finally.

"You must return to the Barbary," Eades said.

"What? Why there?"

"Because it is the only place where you won't be taken up as mutineers and pirates. The word's already spread from those crewmen you released on Kuriyya, and *Minorca's* identity is now well known throughout the border systems. To the Republic, as well, even Hanover — the Marchant reach is long, at least when there's no war on, and I'd expect you'll be wanted in *Hso-hsi* as well, before too much time has passed. They'll have put a rather large price on your head, you see?"

"They can't do that," Avrel whispered.

Kaycie laid a hand on his shoulder and squeezed hard.

"We're done, Jon," she whispered. "You can see that."

Eades nodded. "Attacking the Marchants is not lightly done, nor quickly. I've been building a case for years, dozens of informants and hundreds of documented instances of their wrong-doing." He glared at Avrel. "Now there'll be loose talk of these events in the Barbary and they'll tighten their ship." He sighed. "I wasn't bloody *ready*, boy."

Avrel flushed. It was his fault, then, that the Marchants wouldn't be brought down by this? No, he couldn't accept that. The alternative would have been to let all those folk, New London spacers, the women from *Völkerhausen*, and those from the Barbary alike, be sent off into slavery — Kaycie herself, perhaps, as who knew what would have happened to her if she were put in-atmosphere on Kuriyya with no ship.

No. He'd not accept that. One did the right thing and bugger the cost to something larger. There was no justification to have let those men and women be set upon Kuriyya, and he'd not take the blame for the Marchant's power over New London.

"So, it's back to the Barbary, then," he muttered.

"And what you'll do there, I've no idea," Eades said. He took a deep breath. "I'll try to help you, from time to time, as I may, but you'll be well-advised to keep clear of the Marchants."

Avrel flushed again, this time with anger. The law would never bring them down, would it? The Marchants would never see justice for what they'd done. His jaw was tight and he raised his gaze to meet Kaycie's. She seemed to read something in that as their eyes met, for she smiled, thin-lipped though it be, and nodded.

"I've a ship, Mister Eades," Avrel said. "Two, if I can find Dary and *Fancy*, as well as guns and a crew with blood in their eye and on their minds." He met Eades' eye and, for the first time, it seemed it was the Foreign Office man who saw something in that gaze to chill him, instead of the other way around.

"We'll see who has the need to keep clear, shall we?"

ALSO BY J.A. SUTHERLAND

To be notified when new releases are available, follow J.A. Sutherland on Facebook (https://www.facebook.com/jasutherlandbooks/), Twitter (https://twitter.com/JASutherlandBks), or subscribe to the author's newsletter (http://www.alexiscarew.com/list).

Alexis Carew

Into the Dark

Mutineer

The Little Ships

HMS Nightingale

Privateer

The Queen's Pardon

Planetfall (prequel)

Spacer, Smuggler, Pirate, Spy

Spacer

Smuggler (coming 2019)

Trade Runs

Running Start (coming 2019)

Running Scared (coming 2019)

Running on Empty (coming 2019)

Short Stories

Mad Cow

Dark Artifice

(Writing as Richard Grantham)

Of Dubious Intent

ABOUT THE AUTHOR

J.A. Sutherland spends his time sailing the Bahamas on a 43' 1925 John G. Alden sailboat called Little Bit ...

Yeah ... no. In his dreams.

Reality is a townhouse in Orlando with a 90 pound huskie-wolf mix who won't let him take naps.

When not reading or writing, he spends his time on roadtrips around the Southeast US searching for good barbeque.

Mailing List: http://www.alexiscarew.com/list

To contact the author:
www.alexiscarew.com
sutherland@alexiscarew.com

Made in the USA
Coppell, TX
06 July 2021